'About this morning...'

Vanessa sat, reluctantly, avoiding Preston's gaze, as she said, 'I'm sorry I barged in. It's a mistake that, having made twice, I shan't repeat again, I assure you.'

'Which is why you've hidden in here all day? Deliberately, to avoid me?' he queried.

'I've been busy, that's all.'

Preston gave a deep sigh. 'Oh, Vanessa, you don't understand—'

'I assure you I do,' she contradicted him icily.

'Hell's teeth, Vanessa, come off that pedestal of yours and try to behave like a human being for once!'

Carol Wood writes her medical romances based on personal experience, backed by her work in medical general practice. Married to a water-colour artist and with three of her children now living on the south coast, she enjoys conservation of wildlife, reading and curio shops.

Recent titles by the same author:

PERFECT PARTNERS
PERFECT PRESCRIPTION
AN OLD-FASHIONED PRACTICE

PRESTON'S PRACTICE

BY
CAROL WOOD

MILLS & BOON®

MILLS & BOON and MILLS & BOON with the Rose Device
are registered trademarks of the publisher.

First published in Great Britain 1997
Harlequin Mills & Boon Limited,
Eton House, 18-24 Paradise Road, Richmond, Surrey TW9 1SR

© Carol Wood 1997

ISBN 0 263 80191 8

Set in Times 10 on 11 pt. by
Rowland Phototypesetting Limited
Bury St Edmunds, Suffolk

03-9706-51755-D

Printed and bound in Great Britain
by Mackays of Chatham PLC, Chatham

CHAPTER ONE

VANESSA stood quite still, her long coppery hair blown gently around her shoulders by the April breeze. Slowly, savouring the taste of salt, she licked her lips. Her grey eyes began to soften as she gazed out over the waters of the bay to the next peninsula in the distance.

The hospital looked as small as a matchbox, lying peacefully bathed in the sun with no indication of its frenetic inner life. Who would have known from this windswept perch that the huge six-storeyed block towered over five other modules set in a hexagon around a small lake? Brideport General had come a long way since she and Tara—her twin—had trained there nine years ago. Newly built then, it had been a little city all of its own and they had lived and breathed its vitality.

Vanessa wondered why she had come to pause here at the little beauty spot before going on to her interview. Coastal East Sussex in spring! Enough to melt anyone's heart, she thought wistfully as she brushed her hair from her face and steadied herself against the southerly wind as it blew against her elegant spring suit, moulding the soft pearl-grey cloth to her body like a glove. She gave a shudder and folded her arms around herself. Something had drawn her to this place—could it be Tara?

'Lost?' asked a deep voice, startling her out of her reverie, and she spun around—to meet a pair of deep green eyes, their lucidity enhanced by a shock of incredibly thick dark hair which was totally unmoved by the breeze. She had been so deep in thought that she didn't think for the moment of how unusual it was for her to look up to— and not into—a stranger's gaze. Her height had made her

5

careless over the years as she rarely needed to tilt her head up, especially when she was wearing heels. In bare feet and in a relaxed posture, she was a generous five-eight. If she pulled herself upright, she added another willowy inch.

So the movement came as a novelty, if barely registered, as she lifted her gaze to smile at him. 'No,' she answered politely, 'thanks all the same. I'm not lost.'

'What a pity.' With a flourish the man finished closing the door of the sleek black car parked next to hers, which she vaguely remembered being parked there as she'd driven onto The Point. 'I was hoping I would be able to air my knowledge of Brideport. Beautiful on a day like this, isn't it?'

Vanessa nodded, her gaze going back to the arc of calm blue sea. 'Very. It's a place you never forget. . .'

'Do I detect some hint of regret,' the distinctively deep voice drawled, 'even an iota of nostalgia?'

She looked back, realising that she was being studied—with an uncomfortable degree of perception—by a complete stranger. He stood with one arm casually draped along the top of the car—which she now identified as a Porsche. And the large, hair-strewn wrist lying on it, emerging from a casual blue sports jacket, revealed a very understated, but very expensive gold wrist-watch.

'Not at all,' she shrugged. 'I was simply taking a breath of fresh air.'

'And here was I, imagining you were a lady in distress and perhaps I could help in some way.'

It was a charming line, she mused, but wasted on her if only he knew it. She wasn't in the least bit interested in striking up a conversation—flattered, yes, possibly, but not interested in anything except getting the interview with Dr Caroline Grey over and done with as soon as possible, and hopefully taking one step nearer to saying goodbye to Brideport and nursing once and for all.

'Thanks for the offer,' she declined, flashing him a

regretful smile, 'but I'm late for an appointment and I really must fly.'

'Oh, dear, what a shame. And just when we were getting to—'

Vanessa lost the rest of his sentence in the breeze as she turned and jumped quickly into her car, wondering with not a little embarrassment what the expression on her face had revealed as she'd gazed across the bay in her dream world, but even before she'd started the engine a solid brown knuckle rapped on the window.

She wound it down six inches. 'Yes?'

'Ah. . .it's strange, but I've a distinct feeling—'

'That we've met before?' she intoned drily, lifting an amused eyebrow.

'Absolutely. Have we?'

'Sorry, not as far as I know.' She rewound the window and, thrusting the car into reverse, jolted backward with a huge screech of brakes which she hadn't entirely meant to make. Seconds later she was roaring off down the hill, feeling a vague sense of annoyance at herself for the rather artless brush-off she'd given him.

'Nothing personal,' she sighed to the lone figure revealed in her driving mirror, dragging her whole concentration back to the interview—her sole reason for her reluctant visit to this part of Brideport.

Turning left at the bottom of the hill, she drew the Citroën up at the modern two-tier building and her grey eyes studied the sign outside on a black plinth—inscribed in large, confident golden letters, BRIDEPORT SURGERY.

She'd had no cause before to come to this recently developed part of town—and, quite honestly, she didn't think that she would be coming here again. Because the agency had been so persuasive she'd agreed to see Caroline Grey, despite her repeated protests that if she was going to stay in Brideport for the summer she wanted work in hospital management and not nursing. Still, she had come this far so she had better find somewhere to park and be done with it.

As she hesitated at a space a loud hoot made her jump and stall her engine. Her mouth dropped open in shock. It was Him again, leaping from the black Porsche which had flagrantly stolen the space she was just about to squeeze into.

He lifted the selfsame knuckle and rapped again on her window. 'What a coincidence!' he mouthed, as though she were deaf.

'Are you by any chance following me?' she demanded, winding down the window irritably.

He shrugged. 'Well, colliding would be more precise, don't you think?'

'You deliberately shot in and took the space I was about to use!'

'That's true.' He narrowed dark eyes over the car park. 'But there's plenty of space left in there. Look, there's one just made for this neat little car of yours.'

'That's not the point. I was here first,' she protested. 'And, what's more, you could have caused an accident. Do you realise you almost hit my bumper in that madcap swerve?'

'Not my fault—you were creeping forward. You couldn't have had your handbrake on.' He peered in, looking at the floor beneath the console.

Vanessa glanced down. The handbrake lay in a horizontal position, yet she was certain that she had pulled it up! How on earth could she not have noticed that she was moving?

'I think,' he said, running a hand through his dark hair, 'before we go any further, I'd better explain something—'

'Don't bother. I'll find somewhere else to park,' she snapped as she started the car and the engine fired into life. 'Now, if you'll excuse me, I'm late as it is.'

Cursing male drivers in general, she accelerated away

and swerved into the car park—deliberately ignoring the vacant space he had just suggested. If he was one of Brideport Surgery's patients the poor doctors had her full sympathy!

Giving him a few moments' start, she glanced back over the car park and was relieved to find the coast clear. Finally she made her way inside the building and checked in at Reception, even more relieved not to see him lurking anywhere.

'Found a space, I hope?' interrupted a by-now-familiar voice as he reappeared—like the genie from the lamp—beside the potted plants. 'Sorry about the. . .er. . .little contretemps outside.'

Vanessa sighed. 'Never mind, it doesn't matter,' she dismissed, and walked across to the magazines—a plain enough hint in anyone's language.

'Well, I think I should introduce myself.' He held out his hand as he came up beside her. 'I'm—'

'Don't you ever give up?' Vanessa felt her jaw dropping.

He laughed softly. 'In your case—no.'

She realised that tact was useless—this man needed a hammer to ram home the fact that she really wasn't interested! 'I really don't—' she began firmly, but got no further as the girl at the desk caught her attention, waving frantically.

'Miss Perry—this is Dr Lynley,' she called, 'standing in for Dr Grey.'

Vanessa blinked her long, dark lashes, jerking her head back to the man standing in front of her—still with his hand extended.

'Caroline's been called away for the afternoon, so I'm afraid you'll have to make do with me,' he said with a shrug. 'Sorry, just one of those things, I'm afraid.'

'But. . .but outside—' she said agitatedly, taking the

hand and feeling five powerful fingers close firmly around it, 'outside, I thought—'

'I was a patient?'

'Yes, I suppose I did.' She retrieved her hand, not altogether sure that it hadn't been crushed. 'I thought. . .well, I'm not sure what I thought. But why didn't you say?'

'I was doing my best, if you recall?'

'But I was expecting to meet a female doctor. I just didn't expect a man. . .I mean. . .someone else.'

'Hopefully, you're not too disappointed?' he chuckled. 'Come on, let's have a proper chat, shall we? Follow me.'

Vanessa found herself walking behind him, watching the broad, swinging shoulders in front of her lead the way and telling herself that she had known it was a mistake to come here from the beginning—and why on earth hadn't she been firm with the girl at the agency and said no decisively?

Once inside his consulting-room, she made up her mind to do just that. She waited for him to face her—which wasn't such a good idea because when he did he was smiling charmingly and his dark eyes twinkled. 'Do sit yourself down.' He gestured to the patient's chair, taking his own and sinking down in it.

'Dr. . .er. . . Lynley,' she began, remaining firmly where she was, 'I really think I'll be wasting your time. To be honest, I've been looking for temporary work until October. Something in management—a private hospital, or a nursing home, or even the General if they had a post going—'

'Whoa!' He held up his hands. 'Don't panic, I've got the message—more or less.' He studied her and nodded slowly, finally shrugging. 'But now you're here why not stay for a moment or two? You might as well. There's nothing to lose, is there?'

Sit in that seat, Vanessa told herself, and you're lost.

All the same she sat, crossing her long legs demurely and promising herself that there was nothing he could say to make her change her mind.

'As a matter of fact, I really did have this odd sensation I knew you up there on The Point,' he began hesitantly. 'Big mistake, though, to ask a woman you apparently have never seen in your life before if you know her.' He laughed softly. 'My apologies, on that score.'

Vanessa lifted her brows. 'It doesn't matter. I'm sorry I was abrupt. But I honestly don't think I recognise you from anywhere.'

She had been so determined to label him a smoothie— more to the point a smoothie who had been deliberately antagonising her up there on The Point—that she had only taken in superficial physical details. Now she looked a little closer and saw that the dark, clean-cut, square-jawed face with grass-green eyes set intelligently apart was a face she would not easily forget.

He shrugged and sat back in the deep leather chair. 'Not to worry. As I understand it, you've come to see Caroline—albeit reluctantly—about filling the practice nurse's post?'

Vanessa bit her lip and sighed again. 'I was persuaded by the agency, you see. They are desperately short of nursing staff at the moment, and in a weak moment...' She shrugged, lifting her eyes expressively. 'In a weak moment I gave in.'

'We are getting a bit desperate,' he told her carefully. 'We've been without a nurse for a month now, which has caused a few ripples. Still, that's not your worry. Look, let's hypothesise for a moment. Just to satisfy my curiosity, would you care to tell me in a few words what you feel— or would feel—you'd have to offer a nursing job in a practice such as this—four doctors, extending catchment area, expanding all the time, cross-section of patients, and so on?' He bridged ten long, supple brown fingers under his chin as he leaned forward.

Vanessa hesitated, reluctant to be drawn, but feeling that she owed him at least this she gave a small shrug. 'Well. . .I believe being a good listener is fifty per cent of nursing. Your patient will usually tell you what is wrong if given enough time—that is, if you allow them to respond in their own way. Forcing the issue of treatment often worries them. . .until they've relaxed and, to a certain extent, come to trust you.'

He nodded, the green eyes moving over her face and causing her to blush again as she heard him prompt, 'And the other fifty per cent?'

She smiled, her eyes lighting up with enthusiasm. 'Oh, that's the practical part, if you like—the easiest and most natural for a woman. Finding something to help ease their discomfort; physically equipping them to deal with their illness, discovering ways to cope and handle disabilities. . .' She paused, thoughtful for a moment. 'And yet this too isn't always a matter of medication or a medical procedure. Sometimes. . .it's a very small action. Making a cup of tea, washing a few dishes—a simple act of caring.' She looked up at him and, aware of his scrutiny and feeling that she had probably said too much, stopped abruptly.

'You're obviously enormously committed to nursing,' he mused, picking up a ballpoint pen and threading it through his fingers thoughtfully. 'Why, in heaven's name, give it up?'

'I have reasons,' she answered briefly and without hesitation, 'but I would rather not go into them.'

For a moment his face merely registered a blank. Then he nodded slowly. 'Well, I'm sure you must have—to be so determined to go against the grain. I wish I were able to change your mind and persuade you to come and work with us. Perhaps Caroline would have done a better job of the interview after all?'

She sat in shocked silence for a moment before she responded. 'But you don't even know what my qualifications are!'

'Oh, yes, I know them,' he told her with a shrug. 'Caroline gave me your CV before she left today. You're twenty-six, left school here in Brideport at sixteen, applied for a post as a nursing cadet with the General and then finished your SRN training in London. You've just completed a senior management course and have something amazingly stressful lined up in the big city—Department Head in Nursing Manpower, or some such inventive new title, isn't it?'

She laughed softly. 'How in heaven's name did you remember all that?'

'Because I thought, as you had taken the trouble to come in for an interview, that the least I could do was to commit a few details to memory.'

'Well, I suppose I should be flattered.' She paused, not daring to meet his gaze, and wondered why she was still sitting here—breaking all the resolutions she had made over the last year to avoid a situation like this.

'Are you sure I can't change your mind?' he persisted gently. 'After all, it's not for ever. There's no real commitment here. And we're not a bad bunch, as GPs go.'

She shook her head in bewilderment. 'I'm sure you're not, Dr Lynley. But, even if I were to fill your vacancy, it would mean you would have to re-advertise the job again in October. It just seems a waste of time to take on someone who is purely temporary for a growing practice like this.'

He lifted one dark eyebrow. 'Well, Caroline's sister is a DN. She's six months pregnant at the moment and says she would like to go back to work after the baby is born if she can find a nanny for the child. Besides, I'd rather have six months of your time than two years of someone less committed.'

Vanessa laughed derisively at herself. 'I didn't think I still was.'

'Perhaps,' he suggested, 'you need to think of this as a kind of cathartic measure? Exorcise all the ghosts of nursing before you embark on your new career?'

'Well. . .' Vanessa leaned back in her chair, 'that's one way of looking at it, I suppose.'

'Can I tempt you into seeing the rest of the surgery? Nothing ventured, nothing gained, as it were.'

She hesitated, aware that a simple 'no' would wind up the interview here and now if she really didn't want the job, but instead, and to her great surprise, she found herself nodding. 'If you've no one else waiting?'

'Not at all. I'm all yours—metaphorically speaking, of course.'

For one second there was a flash of something excitingly disreputable in the glimmering green eyes, and she seemed to have difficulty in dragging her gaze away as a shiver of apprehension ran along her spine.

In the end she muttered a businesslike, 'I'll follow you,' though he turned the tables immediately by cupping her shoulders lightly as he moved her gently out of his path to open the door to the hallway for her. Another absurd bolt of sensation ran down her spine but she managed to find her way past him, smiling as though she were unaffected and composed and not feeling as though she were treading thin air under her feet.

Feet which managed to take her through modern, open-plan consulting-rooms, divided into office and examination facilities, and outside into the garden with its casual splashes of colour outside the windows from the creative little flower-beds surrounding neatly tended lawns and benches.

Most of all she liked the humorous, charming, fair-

haired Mike Shelley—the third doctor of the practice—
who immediately put her at ease with horrendous stories
of his adolescent family.

After briefly meeting the two receptionists Val and
Tina—who were too busy with patients to say more than
a brief hello—her guide took her through the clinic rooms,
one of which would be appointed to the practice nurse.

'We're a straightforward enough practice,' Preston
Lynley announced as they came full circle back to his
consulting-room. 'Mike's interest is small ops, of which
we do a fair few here now. Caroline's fancy is obstetrics
and mine is sports medicine—a little penchant I happened
to have developed whilst I was in the States. Caroline and
I have great hopes for the future. We were at university
together, lost touch for a bit whilst I was in America and
then got together to form the practice—something we'd
often talked about in training, but never imagined we
would ever do.'

'Got together.' An interesting choice of words, thought
Vanessa as she watched him, trying to fathom out his
true feelings towards Caroline Grey—although she found
herself sadly defeated as his green eyes came down swiftly
to meet hers.

'Well, what do you think?' His question was direct, and
she knew that she would have to give him an equally
direct answer. First, though, she must ask herself why she
was doing this. She supposed she could blame Charlie!
Charlie was the one who'd persuaded her to put her name
down with the agency, suggesting that she stay for the
summer as an extended working holiday before returning
to London. . .

'I take it,' the voice said curiously, 'the answer is no?'

Vanessa felt a rush of confusion, but then found herself
saying the words she would have thought impossible an
hour ago. 'As a matter of fact, it's not. If you're happy with
my CV and a temporary commitment, I'd like the job.'

'Then you have it,' he told her immediately. 'Welcome aboard, Vanessa.'

And she realised, as she managed an uneasy smile, that out of the two of them she was probably the more surprised.

'A practice nurse for six months!' Charlotte Wentworth tugged her blue uniform dress over her head and grinned. 'Brilliant!'

'Is it?' Vanessa sank down on the sofa. 'I still don't know whether I've done the right thing.'

'Of course you have,' Charlie muttered, thrusting a brush through her short, wavy, fair hair. 'Anyway, what's six months? It'll fly by.'

Vanessa looked up with a sigh. 'It's not the time factor, really. It's just going back to nursing, that's all—even for a short while.'

'And I suppose being chatted up by big green eyes and a philandering smile has got nothing to do with your sudden change of mind?'

'Of course not!' Vanessa tossed back her red-gold head of hair and glared at Charlie. 'One thing I don't need at the moment—'

'Is a man?' Charlie supplied playfully. 'Don't you think a sun-soaked carefree summer is the perfect opportunity to enjoy yourself for once?'

Vanessa smiled ruefully. 'You sound like a travel brochure!'

Charlie clipped on her black belt and studied herself in the mirror. 'You could do worse than a holiday, you know. All those years of looking after your dad and Tara like an old mother hen. Now you've no excuse not to start living your life, and what do you do? You go and bury yourself in a career which is going to demand just as much of you as your family did.'

Vanessa was not offended by her friend's less than

tactful remark. If anything, Charlie was the only one of their crowd who seemed to have no inhibitions about recalling her twin. Most of their friends seemed to have relegated Tara's memory to a safe distance and, Vanessa supposed, she couldn't blame them.

It was their shared profession—nursing—which had, after Tara's death, made Vanessa alter course to management. Nursing had been all they had ever wanted to do. As little girls, she could remember them twisting the arms off their dolls and setting them back in splints and slings. Nursing had been a shared life line for them, despite Tara's bouts of deep depression after their mother had died.

But, when Tara had gone, nursing had also been the most painful reminder. And so Vanessa had decided to switch to management, if only to herald a new phase in her life. If she couldn't quite give up nursing altogether, she had decided, she could at least make a detour.

She sighed at the pang of memory. The riding accident had been such an unlikely happening—Tara caught in a freak storm on the downs, the horse bolting and throwing her fatally. . .

Vanessa determinedly brought her thoughts back to Charlie, who was slipping on her sensible black ward shoes. Who ever would have believed that Charlie Wentworth would become a ward sister? Her friend loved to let her hair down when she wasn't nursing, and Vanessa's smile deepened as she reflected on the thought of the sometimes hilarious moments in training together— which luckily had managed to offset the equally desperate ones when qualifying seemed an impossible dream in those early days.

And now here they were, both at twenty-six, with careers ahead of them that they had never even in their wildest dreams thought possible. Charlie, who had been as mad as a March hare, was now en route to the top of a nursing career at Brideport General and she, Vanessa, was going to attempt a formidable new challenge in senior management in the city.

'I'll find a flat for the next six months,' Vanessa said suddenly. 'I can't monopolise your spare room for much longer, Charlie.'

'And if you dare do that I shall never speak to you again, Vanessa Perry,' her friend snarled. 'Your contribution to the rent these last few weeks is part of my ticket to Spain. And I'm determined to have a holiday, even if you're not!'

Both girls laughed, easy in their long friendship. Vanessa stood up to push Charlie's overflowing shoulder-bag into her arms. 'If you're absolutely sure, then?'

'Positive. Just as long as,' Charlie warned seriously, 'you take life a little less seriously for the next six months and enjoy the summer. Tara is gone, Van. Two years now. You couldn't have prevented the accident. Whether you were here or in London, it wouldn't have made any difference. Now, for once, just try to relax and live a little.'

Vanessa listened patiently, half-prepared for the lecture. Charlie was probably the only one left from the old days who cared enough now to give it.

'Anyway,' Charlie grinned as she walked to the door, 'when do you start this new job of yours?'

'Next week, the Tuesday after Easter Monday.' Vanessa watched relief spread over her friend's face.

'Perfect!' Charlie giggled as she went out, 'We can let our hair down over the weekend. I'm free for thirty-six wonderful, crazy hours!'

When Charlie had zoomed off to hospital in her renovated orange Beetle Vanessa made herself coffee and stared out through the bay window of the cosy little flat. It was a view she had missed dearly, living in London. She could just see over the roofs of the town centre to the tip of St Paul's spire in Denton Avenue, the church she'd attended with Tara in their childhood.

Inevitably, as she stared at the spire, the memories

flooded back. After their mother had died when they were ten, Vanessa, as the elder twin, had taken over Tara's supervision—not easy with the unpredictability of Tara's moods. With Dad trying to hold a job down and look after them, it had sometimes seemed a miracle that they'd coped. But somehow they had for the next six years— Dad, Tara and herself, all in the house at Denton Road.

The tiny grey needle pointing into the sky made her eyes mist. She shouldn't do this, she knew. Charlie had forbidden her to get maudlin. Now the house had been sold. Dad had remarried and lived in Canada with his new wife. All the old crowd from school had moved on. . . Yes, she should get her memories in perspective. And wasn't that why she was leaving Brideport in October— to leave them all behind? She was sensibly quitting the profession that she and Tara had shared so passionately, and was finding new challenges. She was sure now that she had made the right decision.

Vanessa realised that she was thinking about the interview with Dr Lynley, and the green, challenging eyes which had vied with hers for a moment when she had refused to disclose her reasons for leaving nursing. But, then, she certainly wouldn't have confided in a man whom she had known for less than a couple of hours—not that he hadn't managed, quite artfully, to persuade her into the temporary job. And, with a little shudder, Vanessa resolved to put the matter out of her head at least for the weekend.

On the following Tuesday morning, with a less than exciting Easter weekend behind her—having spent most of it shopping, walking and talking late into the nights with Charlie—Vanessa drove to Brideport Surgery.

In Reception she saw Val Watts, one of the receptionists whom she had met previously, and found that she had prepared her list for the morning, with one blood pressure check already waiting.

'Good luck,' Val grinned. 'If you need anything, give me a call. You know your way along?'

Vanessa nodded. 'I do. Thanks.'

'Vanessa?'

She recognised the voice instantly. 'Good morning, Dr Lynley.'

He smiled down at her. 'Do you think we could drop the formalities now? The name is Preston or Pres, whatever's easiest for you.'

As soon as he said the name Vanessa felt that she knew it. But she had never seen him in her life before last week—of that she was absolutely certain. But the name— such an unusual one—rang a bell and yet she couldn't pinpoint it.

'I'm taking surgery until twelve. If there's a problem I'm here to help.'

She nodded and turned to walk along the corridor to her room, but she was hardly aware of where she was going. That name! She was sure she knew it!

Her uneasiness deepened as she walked into her room. She stood stock-still. Preston. . .Pres. . .somehow the name echoed in the shadows of her past, although she could swear that she had never seen him before in her life.

Then it came, piercingly bright into her mind. She sank into the nearest chair, the life draining from her legs. Slowly she bent down and picked up her bag. In the small side pocket she took out an envelope, which had lain against the smooth leather of her bag for two years.

She drew out the letter with trembling fingers and read almost desperately the first crumpled page. When she came to the second page she had to stop and take a deep breath. She had found it—in black and white—in Tara's handwriting.

Vanessa swallowed, closed her eyes and held onto the desk in front of her. All the loose ends which she had never been able to tie up because of Tara's reluctance to explain—here were the answers, right under her nose, and she hadn't realised.

'Nurse, are you free to see me?' someone called behind her and she turned, stuffing the letter back in her bag.

She stood up shakily. 'Yes, of course. Please come in.'

The elderly man, a Mr Crockett—so his notes revealed—tottered across the room and rolled up his shirt-sleeve, well practised in the preparation for his monthly blood pressure check and change of dressing on his leg.

'Nice to see a pretty new face,' he grinned as Vanessa professionally geared herself into action and unwrapped the sphygmomanometer. She folded the cloth around his arm and managed a smile, still distracted by what she had discovered.

She took the reading and wrote it in her patient notes, listening to his amiable chatter. Finally she assisted him onto the bench and began to unwrap the bandaging sur-rounding the varicose vein.

'Oh, that's nice,' the old man said, as Vanessa gently applied a fresh Granuflex dressing. 'You're so gentle. Whilst they've had no nurse the doctors have done it.'

Vanessa smiled. 'I'll bandage the ulcer as carefully as I can. What does the doctor say about it?'

'Oh, I haven't seen him because I'm going to the specialist next week. A pity because I shall miss seeing you.'

Vanessa helped him up. 'Well, there will be your next blood pressure check. I'll look forward to a chat then.'

'It's a date,' chuckled Mr Crockett, shaking down his trouser leg. 'And much as I like chatting with Dr Lynley, I'd much rather see you.'

Vanessa laughed softly at his joke, but when she had seen her patient out she sat down and tried to stop the feeling of light-headedness that almost overcame her as she thought of Preston Lynley—alias Tara's Dr Pres!

CHAPTER TWO

'IT CAN'T possibly be him.' Charlie carefully curled the glazed strawberry back onto the cream dimple of the rum baba with her finger. 'It's just too much of a coincidence, Van.'

'But he thought he knew me from somewhere,' Vanessa insisted, 'and although Tara and I weren't identical twins there was a resemblance, even though she wore those John Lennon specs.' She played with her spoon, finally letting it drop to the table with a noisy clatter. 'Besides, how many GPs are called Dr Pres? Look, this letter from her confirms it.' She displayed the letter once more over the table.

Charlie nodded, sighing, having been forced to read it several times. 'It is a bit weird, I'll admit.'

'Weird? It's positive proof,' Vanessa retorted breathlessly. 'She writes that he was the only one who had identified her childhood riding injury properly and that he had persuaded her to have private treatment with him, for which she needed a loan. That's why I gave the money to her, Charlie. I really did think it might help.'

Charlie swallowed the last morsel of gooey sponge. Heaving a sigh, she frowned. 'Look, what if it is him? There's no point in delving into the past.'

Vanessa was not listening. 'He told me he has a special interest in sports medicine. His name is Preston, shortened to Pres. What more evidence do I need?'

'Evidence? Proof?' Charlie looked exasperated. 'You sound as if you're in a court of law! Look, Van, take my advice. What Tara did with her own life was her business. Even if you don't think much of this guy, she did. It was her choice, not yours. And by raking up everything after two years you won't bring Tara back.'

After a small silence Vanessa shook her head. 'Tara wrote that he had promised she would be fit to ride again. He was giving her treatment. It's in black and white here.'

Charlie's tone became impatient. 'Tara was crazy about horses, but she was scatty too. She wouldn't wear a hat half the time, and the accidents she had were because she took risks. That's why the last one killed her. If she was going through one of her depressions there's no telling what she might have done.'

'But he would have taken X-rays,' Vanessa protested once more. 'He must have known she had spinal cord injuries—how weak her spine was—yet he told her she could ride again.'

'Vanessa, you were not responsible for Tara—you were just her twin. No one forced her on a horse that day. She was riding alone and in terrible weather and without a hat. And going over all this is just self-inflicted torture.'

'But I should have felt—sensed—something was wrong.' Vanessa felt the tears prick at the back of her eyes. Charlie had not seen Preston Lynley. If she had, she would know the kind of man he was and how easy it would have been for Tara to fall under his spell. It wouldn't have been difficult for him to persuade an impressionable young woman into courses of treatment which could only raise false hopes.

They cleared the table and settled themselves down for the evening. Charlie rang Ken, her boyfriend—a doctor at the hospital—and chatted on the phone for what seemed an eternity. Vanessa pressed her uniform for the following day, wondering just what she was going to do about the job. After much soul-searching, by the time she went to bed that evening she had made a firm resolve. If she was going to work at Brideport Surgery then she would use

the opportunity to discover just what bearing Dr Preston
Lynley had had on her sister's death.

It was not a hard resolution to keep once she had managed
to get through one day without looking at Preston Lynley
as though he were an axe murderer.

During the week she met Caroline Grey, an attractive,
dark-haired woman of Preston Lynley's age. Through talking to her, Vanessa deduced that she was very comfortable
with her single status and devoted to her work. Vanessa
was, however, still unsure of the relationship between
Caroline and Preston. All she knew was they had trained
together and that after Preston's return from America five
years ago they had formed the practice between them,
inviting Mike Shelley in when the practice began to take
off. Vanessa could not imagine that the sultry Latin looks
of Caroline would not, at some point, have attracted
Preston Lynley's personal attention.

On the following Monday morning Vanessa had just made
herself at home in her room when her first patient walked
in. He was a tall man, wearing black motorbike leathers,
and would have had two piercing blue eyes—had one not
been a very sore-looking red.

'I seem to have got something in it,' he explained
miserably. 'Probably from the ride to work on my
motorbike.'

When he had settled himself on the examination couch,
she washed her hands and examined the offending eye with
her ophthalmoscope. Donning sterile gloves, she pulled the
lower lid down gently and, finding it clear, curled the top
lid over a sterile swab and searched once more. 'There's
nothing in there now,' she reassured him, 'but it's rather
bloodshot. You must have injured the tiny blood vessels.
I'm going to wash the eye for you to make sure it's clean.'

She carefully cleansed it with an optical wash and

offered him an eye guard to wear, but he insisted that he would manage without one. 'How are you on backaches, Nurse?' he teased her.

She gave him a wry grin. 'Why? Have you got one?'

'Would I get a massage if I said I thought I had a slipped disc?'

She laughed softly. 'No, you would have a great deal of pain and I would send you in to see one of doctors.'

'In that case, I think I suddenly feel very much better,' he grinned, and got up to go.

As they parted Tina, the second of the two young receptionists, put her head around the door. 'Vanessa, I've another young man outside who's just come in. Tim Robson. He doesn't have an appointment. He says he wants to see a nurse for a simple support bandaging. You haven't anyone waiting at the moment. Will you see him?'

'Yes. . .have we any records for him, Tina?'

'We're just checking on the computer.'

Tim Robson limped in, accompanied by a young woman whom he introduced as his girlfriend. She seemed rather shy and Vanessa smiled at her as she sat beside him, noticing how pale and thin she looked.

'I think I pulled a ligament at yesterday's match. I wonder if you could strap it up for me?' Tim asked, cautiously extending his leg.

'Did this happen during football?' Vanessa asked, seeing how stiff it was.

'Yeah, a charity match. Season's over for a bit.'

'Perhaps we'd better take a look on the bench, I think.' She helped him from the office, smiling at the girl. 'Who normally sees you?' she enquired as, in the treatment room, he slid his trouser leg down.

'Dr Lynley. . .ouch!' He sank onto a chair, instantly reluctant to swing his leg on the bench.

Vanessa felt a twinge of dismay as she examined the muscle on the thigh he was holding. The knee was heavily swollen. 'I think I had better let the doctor have a look,' she murmured. 'Have you had any trouble with the kneecap before?'

He nodded. 'A bit. You know what football's like. The doc gave me exercises to do. Thought it might be a cartilage or something.'

Vanessa left him to go in search of Preston Lynley, stopping on the way to talk to Tim's girlfriend. 'Tim needs to see a doctor,' she told her. 'He's obviously in a great deal of pain, and I can't do much—not without the doctor's authority.'

The girl nodded and stood up slowly. 'I'll go and read some magazines in the waiting-room.' She hesitated, staring at Vanessa with huge, dark-ringed eyes. 'Actually, I wanted to ask you something—' But she stopped short as Tina knocked on the door and handed Vanessa Tim's records, explaining that Preston was free.

'I won't keep you a moment,' Vanessa apologised, and moved to the internal phone to make the call. 'I have a patient of yours with me, Preston. Tim Robson? Could you take a look at him for me, if you've a moment spare?'

'The footballer?'

'He's complaining of a thigh injury, but I don't like the look of his knee. I don't want to put on a support bandage if it's anything more than a sprain.'

'OK. I'll be there.'

When Vanessa looked up the girl had gone. For a moment she debated whether to go after her, but just then Preston appeared.

'Let's have a look, shall we?'

Vanessa followed him to the small room. Her eyes ran over the tall figure, striding before her, which exuded a kind of natural energy as he moved—broad shoulders encased in a trendy collarless burgundy shirt, slim hips tapering to long cord-clad legs.

The effect was pretty dazzling, and not what you would

expect to see sitting opposite you on a Monday morning
when you went to complain about your flu bug, Vanessa
decided, trying to reassemble her thoughts as she stood
beside Tim.

'Hi,' Preston greeted him. 'What have you been up to
lately?'

'Chance would be a fine thing,' muttered Tim
miserably. 'Can't do a thing with this leg.'

Preston shone one of the examination lights on the knee,
and glanced at Vanessa. 'Most of the trouble seems to be
in the patellofemoral articulation and shows up in the area
just below the knee. . .here.' The kneecap was obviously
giving signs of stress, and as the long, gentle fingers
smoothed the swollen skin Tim gave an involuntary wince.

'I thought you were resting this for the summer?'
Preston frowned.

Tim reddened. 'Got persuaded into a game yesterday.
More fool me.'

Despite a disparaging grunt of disapproval, Vanessa
noticed how Preston's strong hands worked thoroughly
and painstakingly over the knee and how, after a suc-
cession of rapid-fire questions with regard to Tim's
supposedly non-existent training sessions, it transpired that
the youngster had indulged in far too much activity since
the last time he had been seen.

Preston did not mince words. 'I'd like to have a look
at the joint with an arthroscope,' he told Tim firmly. 'With
this particular technique we can diagnose a joint injury
and perform an operation through a tiny incision, rather
than conducting major surgery. In my view, it would be
too risky to leave any longer.'

Tim groaned loudly. 'But that will mean I'll be out of
action for weeks, won't it?'

Preston was about to answer when Tina called from the
door of the office. 'Mrs Lithgow for you, Vanessa. And
two more waiting.'

'I'll use the examination room upstairs if you like,' Vanessa offered tactfully. Bye, Tim, and good luck with the knee.' She hurried out to organise a treatment room upstairs for her smears.

Her first patient, Mrs Lithgow, had come for a second test. Vanessa saw that Caroline Grey had asked for Mrs Lithgow's smear to be repeated as there had been a doubtful result from the laboratory on the one she'd had four weeks previously.

'Do you think it's very serious,' Mrs Lithgow asked Vanessa, 'for them to call me back in again?'

'I think probably there were not enough cells in the last test to give a conclusive result,' Vanessa told her unworriedly. 'Pop up on the bench and we'll have another try.' She endeavoured to insert the speculum as gently as possible, but her patient seemed unusually tense.

'You don't think it's cancer of the cervix or anything like that, do you?' The woman stiffened again and Vanessa found that she was unable to take the smear.

'What makes you think that, Mrs Lithgow?'

'Oh, you hear so many things on TV and, to be honest, when I had my last smear, it hurt a bit, although I didn't like to complain.'

'I think it hurt,' Vanessa told her gently, 'because you tensed up—as you are doing now—and then the speculum sometimes becomes uncomfortable between the muscles. I promise I shall try to be very careful. Now, will you do something for me? Lie back and relax your body, just letting go of all your thoughts for the moment. Wiggle your toes and fingers and take a deep breath from the pit of your stomach, exhaling very slowly and simply concentrating on your breathing.'

It took a while to encourage her patient into a relaxed posture before Vanessa attempted to take the smear again. Wanting to make this experience pain-free, she waited until Mrs Lithgow was involved in her breathing, then slipped the speculum in without difficulty and gathered the sample on the spatula.

'Well done,' Vanessa encouraged and withdrew the speculum, setting the sample aside for labelling. 'I'm sure there won't be a problem with this one.'

'I didn't hardly feel you,' Mrs Lithgow said in surprise, easing herself from the couch. 'That breathing helped me, I think.'

'Why not invest in some relaxation cassette tapes?' Vanessa suggested. 'They really are very helpful, or even a course of yoga at night school?'

Mrs Lithgow nodded. 'Perhaps I will. I do get very uptight sometimes. You've got me thinking now.'

Vanessa smiled. 'Which is a nurse's job, isn't it?'

Mrs Lithgow collected her bag and hesitated, lowering her voice. 'You've got a nice, gentle manner, dear. And you bothered to talk to me about the smear. It makes you feel human when someone does that.'

Vanessa saw her patient off, trying not to think how fulfilled she felt when someone said something like that. It was the one-to-one contact she would miss dearly when she went into management—the personal rapport which made the job so worthwhile.

Trying not to think about it for too long, she returned downstairs to find that Preston and Tim had disappeared. With a little shiver, she could still discern the musky scent floating around the room that was very definitely Preston Lynley. As she was thinking of him, he appeared at her door. 'Busy morning?'

'Steady.' She raised her brows. 'And Tim?'

'He's still indecisive. The lad's reluctant to have it looked at, worrying that it will put him out of action completely for the summer. But one way or another something will have to be done.'

She paused, tilting her head thoughtfully. 'When you suggested a clinical inquiry, would you do it yourself?'

He shrugged as he walked towards her and perched a thigh on the corner of her desk. 'Why, don't I look the type?'

She was taken aback. 'No, I didn't mean to suggest you couldn't attempt an investigation—'

'Didn't you? I wonder. I wonder what you really think I'm capable of.'

'You're a doctor,' Vanessa said, flustered, feeling the atmosphere change as she coloured in embarrassment at the truth of his words. 'And I'm sure you're a very capable doctor—'

'It's nice to know I have your confidence,' he cut in abruptly. 'You know, I thought you might warm a little towards me—treat me with less suspicion that you did at first—but I've a feeling you're even more distant now than you were the day I met you up there on The Point.'

Vanessa blushed as she realised that she must be allowing her emotions to show through. She had never been very good at hiding her true feelings, something Tara had often hurled at her during one of their disagreements.

'Anyway,' he said before she could think of an answer, 'to go back to your question—I will probably ask a colleague of mine at Brideport General to see Tim. The lad has been in trouble with his knee for almost a year now and the physio he's been seeing—a private consultant recommended by his club—hasn't helped at all.' He slid off her desk and thrust his hands into his pockets. 'Do you mind if I ask why all this sudden interest in Tim's case?'

She shrugged. 'No special reason. Sports are an interest of mine too, as it happens, and. . .er. . .the thought struck me that someone might want a referral for private treatment,' she added inconclusively, hoping she might draw him on the subject.

'For private medicine?' he repeated doubtfully, his gaze narrowing. 'I doubt it. Most youngsters I come into contact with couldn't afford it. If they've a sports injury they come to see me in surgery.'

Another blank. She sighed inwardly, aware of the slightly rougher edge to his voice and the fact that he was frowning down at her as though he couldn't quite decide whether she was being downright nosy or simply obtuse.

'If that's all, then?' She got up and walked from her desk to the door, only relaxing when she was almost in the corridor. But to her dismay, just as she walked away he caught hold of her arm. 'You know, I really do feel I know you from somewhere. . .'

'In another lifetime?' she joked, but was met with clear green eyes that seemed most unamused, perhaps even frustrated, at her pun.

'Maybe,' he shrugged. 'Well, I suppose I had better let you get on.'

'And I you,' she answered, secretly shaken at the discerning stare which seemed to penetrate right through her as she walked away.

As the days passed, Vanessa relaxed. A little.

She liked all the staff and noticed how smoothly things ran. Beth, the practice manager, was a treasure and always helped her with any queries, seeming to know everyone on the register. And, apart from the one hiccup with Preston, she avoided any more head-ons whenever she could, consulting either Mike or Caroline who were always happy to help.

By the time she had cause to speak to him again it was almost half past four on a sumptuously warm Friday afternoon in May. A woman had come in at the last moment with her little girl and asked if she could see a member of staff, and Val had approached Vanessa. 'Have you a moment?' she asked hesitantly. 'We've no doctor on the premises at the moment, and Mrs Searle says Katie is running a temperature.'

'Of course.' Vanessa smiled at Katie, who sat on her mother's lap and did indeed look very flushed. 'Will a doctor be back should I need to refer Katie?'

'Dr Lynley should be,' Val responded uncertainly. 'But he could be half an hour, could be two.'

Vanessa nodded and introduced herself to mother and daughter. Katie was five, a small, fair-haired girl with beautiful blue eyes. She looked fevered and Vanessa was not surprised to find her temperature was high, but what concerned her equally was a spreading rash on the child's arm. 'Has she a rash anywhere else?' she asked Mrs Searle, who removed Katie's dress and cotton slip to reveal a bright red rash developing over her chest.

'Measles?' asked Mrs Searle.

Vanessa did not think it was, but hesitated to say so. The rash was mainly on the arms and it was not the flat, dark pink spots that joined together as was synonymous with measles. Also, she was dismayed to find swollen glands in Katie's neck and under her arms. 'I'm just going to listen to your chest,' she told the child with a reassuring smile. 'Would you like to take a deep breath for me?'

Katie complied. But she had a cough, and after a while she turned her head back into her mother's chest and would not be examined.

'She's been under the weather for quite a while,' Mrs Searle said, managing to re-dress Katie. 'And then when I saw the spots I thought she might be sickening for German measles.'

Vanessa said that it would be best for the doctor to check her and that she would ask him to call this evening as he had not yet arrived back at the surgery. In the meantime, she suggested that Katie be tucked up in bed until he arrived. 'Have you any transport?' she asked as an afterthought.

Mrs Searle shook her head. 'We came on the bus straight

after school. They had rung me to say she wasn't very well. Perhaps I'll call a taxi.'

Vanessa glanced at her watch. 'I'm off duty now so I'll give you a lift, if you like. I see you live in Howarth Road. That's only a few streets away from where I live in Chandler's Row.'

Mrs Searle hesitated, but finally accepted. After writing down the visit in the book and telling the receptionists, Val and Tina, what was happening, Vanessa drove her two passengers home. Ten minutes after they had arrived there was a knock at the door, and Vanessa answered it to Preston.

'Problems with Katie?' He lifted one dark eyebrow and she thought she detected a flash of warmth in the green eyes, but it soon disappeared as she began to explain what had happened.

'Hi, Katie,' he called as they walked into the bedroom, and the little girl stared up with wide blue eyes set darkly in her highly flushed face. He perched on the bed, flipped open his case and chuckled. 'Do you fancy having a listen through the stethoscope again?'

Katie nodded and reached out, and her mother touched Vanessa on the arm. 'While Dr Lynley is examining her, I'll make us some tea.'

Vanessa followed her out of the room, intending to say that she wouldn't stop now that the doctor was there. She certainly didn't want to cramp Preston Lynley's style after what had been said before between them over Tim's case. But the older woman spoke as they went downstairs. 'It was very kind of you to give us a lift and to stay and talk to Katie. I hope we haven't made you late for your meal.'

Vanessa frowned. 'You mean my beans on toast? No, I think the tin will keep for another hour or two.' They laughed together and Vanessa ventured a guess. 'I take it Katie knows Dr Lynley pretty well?'

'Oh, yes, he's wonderful with her,' Katie's mother

responded instantly. 'She's had a year of poor health, but he's helped us to muddle through somehow. It's a pity she hasn't any brothers or sisters to keep her company, but John and I tried for more and they never came along. Still, that's the way it goes sometimes.' She glanced up towards the bedroom. 'I miss her rather a lot now she's started school.'

From the sounds of the giggling that wafted down the stairs, Katie was lapping up the attention and they both laughed again. 'He's got quite a way with kids,' Mrs Searle remarked and just as she was about to go through to the kitchen a pair of long, cord-covered legs came down the stairs.

'Temperature is still up a little,' Preston said, appearing not to be unduly worried. 'The rash is rather puzzling, though. Has she been complaining about anything else?'

'Well, now you come to mention it, for a long time she had said her legs feel tired and stiff and she wants to sit down.'

Preston nodded. 'Well, not to worry. I'll call in again tomorrow—and, oh, yes, I've taken a blood sample just as a precautionary measure, as with all children. My advice for now is to keep her quiet and comfortable. Should her temperature rise I would like you to ring me. Otherwise, plenty of fluids and feed her what she likes—you know the procedure by now.'

'Oh, yes, that I do. Are you sure you both wouldn't like a cup of tea?'

Preston said that he must leave and Vanessa declined too. 'What do you think?' she asked as they closed the garden gate behind them. 'Katie seems most concerned with her joints, not particularly with the rash or the glands. Could it be a viral infection, do you suppose?'

'Possibly. But somehow. . .I think not.' He stood still, lost in thought. 'She has had quite a bad patch of ill health over the past year. All the more reason to get the path lab to check out this sample swiftly. Too late now, but I'll drop it off first thing.' He glanced at his watch. 'Anyway, I must go. I've another call in the next road.'

Vanessa watched him jump into the Porsche and move out from the kerb, taking off in a quiet purr of acceleration without even glancing back at her.

Well, that was that, she supposed. She must have upset him more than she'd thought. But it really was the strangest of sensations when she was near him. An awareness, almost a prickle, washed over her that was sometimes difficult to ignore in his company, but this very response made her even more determined to keep him at a distance. She couldn't quite get the whole thing in balance.

As she drove home she recalled what Mrs Searle had said. He was, it seemed, a popular doctor with his patients, and with children especially. But, then, what had she expected from Preston Lynley? A cloaked, shadowy figure who roamed the streets at night and whom she could label quite clearly the villain of the piece, just because Tara had had some form of involvement with him?

Vanessa sighed and tried to put Preston Lynley from her mind for the rest of the evening—at least.

She was dressed in a rainbow-hued T-shirt and black leggings an hour later, with her hair cascading in fiery tangle around her face as she tried to prise open a tin of sardines—having found no beans—when the front doorbell pealed.

It couldn't be Charlie, she thought, for she had just phoned to say that she was on a late duty and then she would be staying over with Ken. Trust someone to call when she was ravenous!

'Who is it?' Vanessa demanded into the intercom, trying to wipe the soya oil from her hands with a cloth and mentally vowing that she would invest in something a little less obstinate to extract from its tin next time she raided the cupboard.

'Me,' said the voice.

She frowned into the tiny microphone, unable to believe her ears. 'Me?' she repeated lamely.

'Preston. May I come up? I shan't keep you long.'

Her dismay escalated to panic. 'I'll come down,' she yelped. She tried the door and her oily hands slid around the handle. 'Oh, hold on a minute,' she called breathlessly. And, ignoring the disturbing spiral of excitement squirming around her spine, she managed to successfully release herself into the hall.

CHAPTER THREE

'MY LAST call, if you remember,' Preston Lynley reminded Vanessa as she opened the door, 'was just around the corner.'

Vanessa hesitated as she inhaled the musky drift of aftershave borne in on the breeze. 'Yes, yes, I do remember, but what—?'

'To be truthful,' he cut in hastily, 'I wanted to thank you.'

'For what?'

He seemed uncertain. 'Well. . .for looking after the Searles, for a start. They've had a rough time of it and you were. . .kind.'

Vanessa let out a sigh of relief that his call meant nothing untoward, and that he seemed to have forgotten their earlier coolness. 'Oh, delivering them home was on my way. It was a pleasure,' she smiled and, before she had time to think, she opened the door wider. 'Would you like a coffee before you go back to the surgery?'

He seemed surprised, but he nodded. 'If it's convenient. Thanks.'

Only just recollecting that she had left the mutilated tin of fish open on the worktop, she stopped halfway up the stairs leading to the flat. 'I'm sorry, but you'll have to ignore the chaos. . .'

'The coffee sounds fine,' he assured her, but on entering the flat he stopped and wrinkled his nose. 'My goodness, what's that?'

'It was my supper.' Vanessa hurried from the lounge to the kitchen, where she scooped the evidence into a plastic bag and thrust it into the fridge. 'Milk and sugar?'

she called as she unsuccessfully began to try to tackle the
mountain of washing-up on the drainer.

'Look, what if. . .' she heard a deep voice say as she
swivelled around to find that he had followed her and was
watching with a frown, 'what if we forget the coffee?
Neither of us has eaten, it seems. How do you fancy trying
some real food?'

Vanessa opened her grey eyes wide, which made her
look rather like a wildcat, with her hair in a flurry around
her face. 'Real food?'

He shrugged. 'Oh, something like fresh avocado followed by pasta filled with spinach, cooked in a cheesy
sauce and topped with garlic?'

She couldn't hide the appreciative rumble her stomach
made at the thought of such a delicious suggestion. 'You
make it sound very tempting. But, as you can see, I'm not
really dressed for dinner, thanks all the same.'

He glanced at his watch. 'I've a few calls to make on
the car phone and my visits to write up. I'll wait for you
downstairs. Just throw on something comfortable.
Cosmo's is very informal, I can assure you.'

'Oh, I don't think—'

But he had already turned, and she watched him disappear from the flat. Shaken by his impromptu arrival and
the sudden invitation to eat, Vanessa stood indecisively
for a moment. Why had she allowed herself to be persuaded? And then slowly she began to calm down and
think a little more clearly, despite the almost overwhelming whiff of tinned fish. She would, perhaps, be able to
discover more about him in a congenial environment, without setting off any alarm bells. This was as good an
opportunity as any, wasn't it? She'd be a fool to ignore
the chance.

Telling herself that this was the only reason her heart
was picking up speed and making her pulse race up to her
throat, she headed for the shower, stripping off as she

went. Lavishing herself with talc afterwards, there came a moment's agony in deciding what not to wear, but finally she dug out of her wardrobe a pair of tartan trousers and a matching grey silk top. Charlie's extra-powerful hairdryer took the wetness from her hair, and she brushed its dampness into a silky, coppery sheen onto her shoulders. Slipping on black pumps and dashing perfume behind her ears, she stroked on a heart of tawny lipstick before she left.

When she arrived at the car she discovered that she had rushed unnecessarily, for the occupant was deep in conversation on his mobile phone. She slid in beside him as he said goodbye to Caroline Grey, turning to her and arching a dark, appreciative brow. 'You look great. . .no. . .very lovely.' The words hung in the air with a sense of sincerity which made her look away and try not to think how elated she felt.

'Aren't you on call?' she asked as he started the engine, wondering for a moment if his good humour had anything to do with the female he had been so deeply engaged in conversation with.

'Just handed over to Caroline. Hungry?'

'Ravenous.'

The Porsche took off in a throb of acceleration. 'Feeding you up,' he said with dry enunciation, 'does something to dispel the miserable vision of you all by yourself in that lonely flat, tucking in to sardines on toast.'

'How did you know it was sardines?' she laughed softly.

'I confess I saw you hide the evidence in the fridge.'

'Oh,' she smiled and looked back to the road, realising that there wasn't very much that missed the astute green eyes. 'And just for the record,' she added drily, 'I don't live all by myself in a lonely flat. I share it with my flatmate, Charlie. And it's a very cosy little place when I have time to tidy it.'

He nodded soberly. 'Oh, I see.'

She wasn't quite sure what he did see, but they travelled in silence once more and she hoped that he wasn't already regretting having felt sorry for her—as he obviously had in the flat—and that the meal wouldn't prove a disaster.

He handled the powerful car with skill and care, she thought in sneaky admiration. He wasn't a fast driver; on the contrary, he drove at a steady, safe pace, seeming to know all the short cuts as they glided along in luxurious comfort.

Presently they came to a triangle of small shops and a restaurant named Cosmo's, squeezed in between a florist which was still open and a block of offices on the other side.

'Not the most salubrious of surroundings,' he apologised, pulling on the brake as he slid the wheels alongside the kerb. 'But I can guarantee you an excellent supper.'

Vanessa sniffed the succulent air as she opened her door. 'Well, whatever, the smells are wonderful.'

He came around and cupped her elbow, steering her towards the tiny restaurant. Cosmo's, she discovered, was not the most sophisticated of restaurants, with its tiny tables and wheel-backed chairs, but it was cosy and the service was personal. As they ate the delicious tortellini Cosmo himself poured the wine, appearing in his chef's hat and white apron.

The Chardonnay was delicious and, although she noticed that Preston drank fruit juice, she indulged in a second glass before her out-of-this world *crème caramel*.

'What's the verdict?' he asked as they finished almost together and he dabbed at the corner of his mouth with a napkin. . .

Her eyes flickered over the sensual lips swept clean by a strong pink tongue and she sank back, her grey eyes avoiding direct contact with the glimmering green ones. 'It was wonderful. Do you eat here very often?'

'Probably more than I should,' he admitted easily. 'But

it becomes a bit of an addiction when going home to prepare a meal seems just a little too much bother at the end of the day.'

Did Caroline Grey share his taste in Italian food? she wondered. Not that she managed to discover very much more about him, as had been her original intention. The first nugget of real information came from Cosmo as he finally served them coffee, and Vanessa thanked him for the delicious meal.

'Nothing is too good for Dr Preston and his lovely lady,' he sighed dramatically, and she blushed as she avoided Preston's amused glance. 'Do you know,' Cosmo went on, 'this man saved my little girl's life? He is brilliant doctor! It is good to see he has so beautiful a *signorina* to share Cosmo's excellent food with.'

Preston lifted a reproving eyebrow. 'Be careful what you say, Cosmo. This young lady is a working colleague, and let me warn you she has a marked aversion to flattery, you old rogue.'

Cosmo dismissed this with a wave of his hand and looked once more at Vanessa. '*Bellissima signorina!*' he sighed, and then with a flourish disappeared to his kitchen.

'What did he mean about his daughter?' Vanessa enquired as she sipped her coffee.

'Cosmo has an inflated idea of my capabilities. His teenage daughter had meningitis about three years ago. I was lucky enough to spot it quickly and she came through. But the credit has to go to the hospital medical team, not me.'

Vanessa wondered if this was false modesty and if she was meant to be impressed by it. But he didn't dwell on it, and began to talk about Katie Searle. 'Any ideas on the problem?' he asked casually.

'I'm not really sure.' Vanessa frowned. 'She's been complaining for some while of aching limbs, then there's the rather odd rash and her temperature was 39.5°C.'

He nodded slowly, twirling a teaspoon around and around in his coffee. 'I wonder. . .'

She watched the preoccupation in his face slowly dissolve as he met her gaze. 'Yes?' she urged. 'You wonder. . .?'

'Oh. . .just a thought. . .but let's wait until the blood results are in—no use in speculating. I'll call by tomorrow and check her. Did you know that Sonia Searle is a widow?'

'No. No, I didn't.' Vanessa was shocked. 'When did she lose her husband?'

'Last year, to cancer. He was only thirty-eight.'

'Oh, I had no idea.' Then Vanessa thought back and recollected how Sonia Searle had not suggested that she phone her husband to pick them up from the surgery, but that she would call a taxi. 'I should have picked it up, I suppose, but Val didn't give me any notes and Mrs Searle didn't say. She even talked about her husband and how they had tried for more children. It was almost as if he was about to come home; as if he was still there.'

'Which is why I'm a little more than concerned. I think she's taken it all rather too well. She didn't have time to grieve properly because shortly after she was widowed Katie started being ill.'

'What a run of bad luck,' Vanessa sighed, inclined to agree on reflection that Sonia Searle, in the circumstances, had appeared overly composed.

'I've been trying to persuade her into bereavement counselling, but I haven't had much luck,' he murmured regretfully. 'But she keeps saying she's fine and she's coping, but Lord knows what's going on inside, though.'

'You mean psychologically?'

He nodded. 'Oh, absolutely. I'm beginning to feel I've overlooked something important and it worries me. If I could persuade her to talk to me more. . .' He shrugged, lifting his broad shoulders. 'But there you are. I shall keep on trying, however.'

'Perhaps it's as well to leave the situation as it is,' she said before she could stop herself.

He looked surprised. 'You can't really think that?'

Vanessa stiffened. 'Why not? Some people guard their privacy zealously. Counselling isn't always the answer.'

'But, as a nurse, surely you would recommend that someone like Sonia be given help? She's Katie to look after, a home to run and a part-time job to hold down.'

'I'm not saying she shouldn't be offered it.' Vanessa felt his stare bore into her. 'Only that it would be wrong to intrude on her life and take away the only emotional crutch she has at the moment. Some people prefer to recover independently, in their own way, in their own time.'

'If you ask me,' he responded bitingly, 'that's a defeatist attitude, and I'm rather surprised you subscribe to it.'

That shook her. Professional attitudes over death and loss were often complex and involved and, since she held such personal beliefs of her own after her mother's and her sister's deaths, she had no intention of sharing her most intimate feelings with a man who would label her a defeatist without knowing anything about her. She realised that having come for the meal had been a mistake, and that it would be sensible to leave now. She bent down to retrieve her bag. 'Thank you for the meal, but I think it's time I went.'

He frowned as she stood up. 'Are you sure I can't persuade you into another coffee?'

'No. . .no. I've had quite enough, thanks. I must get home now or Charlie will be wondering what's happened to me.'

The green eyes narrowed for a second, then he stood up. 'I'll not be long,' he said, and she assumed that he had gone to pay. He was away a little longer than she would have expected, and her sense of disappointment and dismay over their altercation grew as she berated herself for having agreed to eat with him in the first place. But she had begun to like him and so to let down that barrier which she had erected in order to protect herself from being hurt in the future.

When he returned to the table Cosmo accompanied him and, unaware of the atmosphere, insisted—rather embarrassingly—on Preston promising to bring her again. It was a relief to reach the car—and even to sit in silence, which was better, she decided, than more hurtful words.

When the powerful Porsche headlights picked out Charlie's block of maisonettes in Chandler's Row she had her hand on the door, all ready to climb out.

'Afraid to talk to me again?' he said as he switched off the engine.

'Again?' She snatched back her hand. 'Why should you think I'm afraid of talking?'

'Doctor's intuition, perhaps.'

'But I'm not your patient.'

'No, you're not,' he agreed. 'But, if you were, I would advise you to relax a little more—just as you no doubt advise your patients, should the need arise.'

Suddenly she thought of her smear patient. 'You're referring to Mrs Lithgow, aren't you? Have you been checking on me?'

He sighed, thrusting a hand through his hair. 'There you go again. Why are you so suspicious? If you want to know, Mrs Lithgow came to me—not I to her—and said how happy she was with the advice you gave her—on relaxation techniques. I didn't sit the poor woman down in a chair and interrogate her, I can assure you.'

The moment she'd said it, Vanessa realised that she had made a mistake. But that was what suspicion did and, remembering Tara, she decided that she had every right to be suspicious. Suddenly aware of how close they were in the small confines of the Porsche and how the sense of intimacy made her feel vulnerable, she once again retreated in to silence.

He sighed, taking her silence for hostility. 'Look, I'd better let you get in to Charlie, I think.'

'Charlie?' She frowned. 'Oh, yes, Charlie.'

'Look, Vanessa. . .' His voice was softer now. She looked up and met his eyes as a shiver of sensation went through her body. Before she could move a long arm crept along the back of her seat and the friction of his touch, light as it was, caused her to draw in her breath.

'Vanessa,' he began again but then, as the bedroom light of the flat suddenly illuminated the grass beneath, he turned to duck and glance upward. 'You'd better go,' he said shortly. 'Charlie seems to be making a point.'

She glanced up at the flat, feeling too unnerved to tell him that Charlie would, no doubt, be in the process of hair-washing and soap-watching. 'I would offer you a coffee, but—'

'But it's late. And I don't think Charlie would appreciate my company as much as yours.' He looked at her from under heavy lids, his green eyes like huge deep lakes of inky water under the frowning brows.

He saw her safely to the pavement, then waited for her to open the outer door of the flats before he drove off. She heard the soft growl of the engine as she stood there, staring at the low, slinky silhouette creeping away between the houses.

In the flat, she slipped off her shoes and walked to the window to draw the curtains, staring forlornly at the space beneath. When Charlie came in from the bathroom, her head and body swathed in towels, she raised her brows and folded her arms, grinning.

'It's not what you're thinking,' Vanessa said, going scarlet.

'And who's to say I was thinking?' Charlie giggled. 'I saw enough from behind the curtains!'

It was a week before Katie's blood results were through.

Beth Foil, the practice manager, handed them to her on a glorious May afternoon when the sun was burning through the glass of the office windows and the blinds had to be drawn against its powerful rays. 'Katie Searle's blood results are back,' she said, catching Vanessa as she paused between patients. 'I think Dr Lynley will want to see her, don't you?'

Vanessa nodded thoughtfully as she studied them. 'Yes,' she sighed, reflecting soberly on the little girl's apparent anaemia. 'I think he will.'

'I'll ring and make an appointment.'

'Thanks, Beth.'

Vanessa walked slowly along to Preston's room, where she found the door ajar. All week she had tried to avoid a meeting, embarrassed by what had happened between them—though, by Preston's indifferent attitude, he hadn't shown that he had paid much attention to the evening at all.

She had her hand on the door when she heard a female voice. Too late to retreat, she interrupted what looked like a very intimate moment between Preston and a patient but then Vanessa stopped, her heart sinking, realising that it was Caroline.

'Vanessa,' he said, dropping his hands, which had been closed around Caroline's arms. 'Come in.'

'I'm sorry. . .you're busy.' She felt dreadful, as though she'd been eavesdropping.

'It's all right, we've finished,' said Caroline, disentangling herself from Preston and brushing her dark hair from her flushed face.

'I just wanted a word about Katie Searle, that was all,' Vanessa floundered as Caroline walked towards her, her eyes revealing something which sent a chill down her spine but she didn't know why. After all, what concern was it of hers what he and Caroline Grey did, even if it was right in the middle of surgery?

'I'm sorry,' Vanessa apologised again after she had gone, 'but the door was open. I had no idea you were...er—'

'Come in, come in!' She had the distinct feeling that he wasn't listening to her, though, as his gaze followed Caroline's retreating form. 'Katie Searle,' he said distractedly. 'Have you seen her blood results yet?'

Vanessa nodded and handed them to him. For a moment their eyes met and then she looked away. Whatever was making her behave like this; why was she feeling such a strange sense of desolation? What business was it of hers if they were having an affair? They were, after all, two single people at liberty to do what they liked.

He sat in his chair, studying the results, oblivious of her thoughts. 'I've decided I'd like her to see a paediatrician, and these results confirm my feelings. He might want a biopsy of the synovium.'

'A biopsy? Why?' Vanessa asked raggedly, desperately trying to drag back her professional concentration.

'My feeling is that she has Still's disease. A juvenile form of rheumatoid arthritis.'

'Still's disease...it's very rare, isn't it?'

'But it explains the anaemia and the rash and the aching limbs. About one child in two thousand ever develops it. I'd like to rule it out, if nothing else. Has she a follow-up appointment?'

'Beth's making her one,' Vanessa explained and then, as he lapsed into a preoccupied silence, she turned to go, feeling that she had to find somewhere to go and hide the distressing ache that seemed to gnaw at her ribs.

'Vanessa?' he called, and she looked back. 'About just now...I think I should explain.'

She stiffened, her cheeks flushing. 'It's none of my

business, Preston. I'm sorry I barged in, that's all. I'm not in the least bit interested in your relationship with Dr Grey, and you certainly don't have to explain anything to me.'

He got up and came to stand beside her, his tall and powerful presence making her shiver as he crooked up one dark eyebrow. 'If I didn't know you better, I would say I'm receiving a rather peculiar signal from you at this moment.'

Although he had been careful to avoid saying it, she knew that he was implying that he thought she was acting as though she was jealous and she blushed in deep humiliation at the thought that he could see so easily into her mind. 'Then I would have to say you're mixing your signals,' she retorted archly, but she knew that her response sounded absurdly pathetic.

He shrugged, studying her with a curious expression. 'Well, if that's the way you want it. . .fair enough. So we shan't talk about Caroline, but I would like to talk about something else—'

Before she had time to answer the internal phone on his desk sounded. He turned back to answer it, but as she moved to open the door and leave he held up a hand and cupped the mouthpiece. 'Hold on, Vanessa,' he called, and she stopped reluctantly. 'Please wait.'

After a few short sentences to the reception desk he replaced the receiver and scribbled a note on the pad. Then he looked up and tilted his dark head. 'Now, where were we?' In a few swift strides he'd crossed the floor and casually propped himself against the door

'I was just on my way out,' she protested, feeling an unsettling warmth wash over her as his arm brushed her shoulder. 'I think we had concluded our conversation.'

'Had we? You know, I really think we should try to get to know one another a little better. Don't you think someone is going to notice the air crackling around us one day?' He gave her a twisted grin.

'I haven't noticed it,' she lied outrageously, lowering her eyes because she didn't have the courage to meet his gaze.

'Then it must be me.'

He was gradually wearing her down—she could feel it. And she didn't trust herself at all these days. Something was happening to her and she couldn't explain her reactions—in fact, she was afraid of her reactions lest she could not control them in his company, like just now when she had walked in on him and Caroline. The thought of him holding Caroline in his arms brought back a fresh surge of pain, and she glanced quickly at her watch. 'I'm afraid I must go,' she said. 'I have one or two things to do this evening.'

'With Charlie?' He looked at her through lowered lids.

'No, as a matter of fact. Tonight, as it happens, I swim.'

'Where?' He looked curious. 'Anywhere I know?'

'At a club. An exclusive club, open to members only,' she told him pointedly. 'Now, if you'll excuse me. . .?'

She could not believe that she was acting like this, running from the room like a frightened rabbit. She could hear the internal phone ringing again, and although his nervous system appeared to be able to take the strain of ignoring it hers certainly couldn't. She avoided the green eyes and flew down the corridor, aching for the cool relief of a swim which would calm the heated rhythm of her heart as it beat furiously against her ribs.

CHAPTER FOUR

VANESSA left the shower and stood on the side of the glittering blue pool, staring at the tall, bronzed figure striding towards her.

Was it an apparition? But no apparition looked so dauntingly male, nor did it walk with the familiar lope she had grown so used to watching over the past few weeks. Except that she had never seen him naked before. Well, virtually naked if you ignored the brief black shorts, clinging wetly to slim brown hips above strong, muscular thighs.

'How did you get in here?' she gasped, shivering from the warm shower which was growing cold on her body.

'By the front entrance, would you believe?' His eyes raked over her simple one-piece powder-blue swimsuit and lingered on the high cut of the leg just a fraction too long to be a respectable scrutiny, before slipping up to her wet, sleekly covered breasts for an equally intensive scan.

'But you're not a member,' she protested, trying to ignore the feeling his inspection was giving her and the multiple goose bumps clamouring revealingly over her skin.

'I'm a guest, having proffered suitable credentials, considering taking out a full membership,' he shrugged, putting out an instinctive protective arm as someone dived in and fountained water across their legs.

Vanessa was torn between anger at him for following her here and a reluctant admiration that he had managed to find her. Centresport was the town's most exclusive and private club, true, but even so his initiative still surprised her.

And if she hadn't kept a very cool head she would now

be drooling madly over the tall, athletic figure standing beside her, just like the group of three young girls in the pool who were giggling up at them.

'Well, shall we swim or would you like to stand here and shiver for a bit longer?' He stepped back, gesturing with a sweep of his hand and making way for her to dive in.

The water was cold at first, but her skilful dive took her to the bottom of the pool and back to the surface just in time to catch the dive he made behind her—skimming the water without a spray, cutting it smoothly and disappearing somewhere beneath her.

She struck out for the other end. Going into her paced breathing, she began a fast crawl. She knew that she could match most strong swimmers for speed, though she was careful in this pool not to mow down anyone and kept a watchful eye ahead of her.

With three lengths of the pool completed, she had just turned for her fourth when a figure bobbed up at her elbow. He gave her a grin and swam effortlessly beside her with long strokes. The more she increased her speed the more he did, although he seemed barely to notice it as every now and then his face turned in the water and amused green eyes met hers. She lost her rhythm and floundered and felt a fool. To cover her embarrassment, she dived under, turned and raced away in the opposite direction.

She was imagining having escaped him when above the noise of the water she heard a clamour. A girl was screaming and others were shouting, and it occurred to her it wasn't someone fooling around because pranks were discouraged in the pool for safety's sake.

Suddenly she found herself a few yards away from the group of girls she had seen earlier. One of them was shrieking hysterically in the deep water and her two friends had disappeared altogether. Vaguely Vanessa registered Preston powering to the spot and a lifeguard just behind him, but before any of them arrived she had already instinctively started to dive.

With strong strokes she bore down, straining her eyes in the blue water. She saw them ahead. One girl in a yellow swimsuit had gone limp with her dark hair floating around her. The other girl was frantically trying to surface, but her panic was dragging her down.

Even before Vanessa had a made a decision on whom to help first Preston's powerful figure appeared, swimming strongly to reach her. He signalled the motionless swimmer and she nodded, pulling herself through the water to slip her arms around the girl.

Almost before she broke surface the lifeguard, after having shouted, 'Clear the pool!', was helping her, and together they gasped for air. All three of them were dragged out of the water by strong hands and Vanessa choked, breathing painfully.

Vanessa struggled onto her knees to watch the lifeguard depress the girl's chest and try to squeeze water from her airways.

Pushing her own wet hair out of the way, Vanessa placed her ear to the cold chest to listen. 'There's a faint heart-beat,' she told him and, taking over, gently tipped back the girl's head, pressed her mouth over the cold blue lips and began to breathe air into the inert body.

'She's going purple,' someone whispered. 'Fetch a doctor.'

'I'm a doctor,' Preston's voice answered as the crowd parted and he knelt down beside her. 'You breathe, I'll pump—OK?' he said as water dripped from his face and body, his muscles flexing as he reached out.

All she could do was nod. Every few moments the terrible picture of the underwater scene flashed before her eyes—the silent, blue water and the girl floating like a piece of abandoned seaweed.

She forced herself to concentrate. Fifteen pumps and

two breaths: Preston's strong hands closing over the breastbone; her own mouth going over the frozen lips, and her silent prayer for help. Down to five pumps and two breaths. The sound of a siren—movement around them— the coldness beginning to stiffen her joints, and doubts forming in her mind as the girl refused to respond.

Two more breaths. Five pumps.

'Breathe,' Preston muttered beside her. 'Come on, come on, breathe for me!'

The scene registered in a kind of dream as the sheer power of his words to the girl seemed to push hope into Vanessa herself. She glanced at his face and saw the determination there, and knew that she was hugely relieved to have him beside her. Then came the hurrying of feet, the shouted instructions and Preston reaching into the bag a paramedic had opened for him.

'Adrenaline,' she heard one of them say, and Preston administered the life-stimulating injection. For a few seconds no one moved and then the first faint response came from the girl as her chest lifted abruptly and her eyelids began to flicker.

'She's back with us,' Preston murmured, and Vanessa felt a surge of almost uncontainable relief. 'Could you check the two other girls for me?' he asked then. 'I think her friend may be in shock.'

She nodded and left them to hurry to the group of people who were clustered on the other side of the pool. In the middle of them sat a girl huddled in blankets, her eyes looking dull with shock. It was the girl in the blue costume whom Preston had saved, together with the friend who had been screaming for help.

'How's Mandy?' they asked almost together as she bent down beside them.

'She's breathing now,' she answered softly. 'The doctor is looking after her.'

'She can't swim very well and she must have gone out

of her depth. I went to help her, but she started to drag me down,' said the girl in blue. 'Then I lost my nerve as she suddenly went all limp in the water.'

Her friend nodded. 'I saw them both go under and I didn't know what else to do but scream.'

Vanessa smiled and pulled the blanket under a very shaky chin. 'Which fortunately got everyone's attention.'

'I feel as though I've drunk the whole baths,' she mumbled, her teeth chattering. 'I probably would have if your friend hadn't come to my rescue.'

Vanessa glanced back to the other side of the pool. Preston was helping to lift the girl on the stretcher, his large body working powerfully to help the ambulance men. 'Do you think you can walk to the changing-rooms?' she asked as she turned back. 'You really should put some clothes on and get warm.'

What she really wanted to do was to get them away from the departure of the ambulance. It would be very upsetting for them to see their friend leaving the place on a stretcher, and both of them were already in a state of shock.

Then she had a little bit of luck. One of the girl's brothers arrived and promised that he would drive them both on to the hospital afterwards. Vanessa went with the girls to the changing-rooms and, after helping them get dressed, saw them into the brother's care and went back to slip a sweatshirt over her damp swimsuit.

The girl on the stretcher was conscious now and Preston slid an arm around Vanessa's shoulders as they watched the little procession move away from the pool. 'How are you feeling?' he asked softly.

'Oh, fine.' But she was shaking and she leaned gratefully against his strong body. The lethargy and numbness was beginning to overtake her. She felt the rumbling vibration of his voice as he told one of the remaining ambulance men how long approximately the girl had been under the water from the moment the alert had gone up, and suddenly the picture of the helpless body in the yellow swimsuit seemed to play before her eyes again.

'Come on, we're going to get you something warm to drink,' Preston told her as she began to shiver. He sat her at one of the pool-side tables and she agreed to drink some tea. When he came back he wore a warm green towelling T-shirt and had bought two strong teas. Over his arm he carried jogging bottoms which were obviously his but he made her stand up and put them on. Vanessa did as she was told, though they were far too big for her.

He held up the cup and she sipped the strong, sweetened tea. 'It's delayed shock, I think,' she mumbled, trying to steady her hands. 'I'm not usually so reactive to a situation.'

He shrugged. 'You don't normally see two people drowning at the same time. Drink up; it'll revive you.' He took hold of her hand and squeezed it, and she found herself hanging onto it and giving him a wobbly smile.

'You're a very fit young woman,' he complimented her. 'We'd swum a dozen lengths or more before that happened and you still managed to drag her up.'

Vanessa bit her lips to bring back the sensation to them. 'I wasn't sure which one to go for first, though. Silly, really. I couldn't make up my mind.'

He gave a small sigh. 'Well, I thought the girl who was struggling might put up a fight and drag you down, so I judged it best for you to handle the other girl. I knew once you had her on the surface you'd know what to do—and I was right, wasn't I?'

She looked up at him and realised for the first time how much trust he had put in her. 'Yes,' she agreed softly, 'but I still don't know if we would have brought her back without the adrenaline. Do you think she'll be all right?'

'Thanks to you, yes,' he smiled, and squeezed her hand once more. 'And, hopefully, she'll never go out of her depth again. It could have been a double tragedy.'

She took gulps of air and dragged them into her lungs. 'Sorry,' she apologised, still shivering. 'I'll be all right in a moment.' But she wasn't entirely sure that she would be, or that her state wasn't due to the way he had compressed her hand in his and was holding it tightly, his shoulder next to hers, so that every now and then their arms touched and the same convulsive response to him shattered her already unnerved equilibrium.

'Have you eaten since you finished work?' he asked, frowning down at her.

She shook her head. 'I don't like to eat before a swim. I usually have my meal afterwards.'

'In that case,' he said firmly, 'I'm going to take you home and feed you. We could both do with something nourishing and then, if you feel fit to drive later, I'll bring you back here to pick up your car.'

She was on the point of refusing when she realised that she really did feel rather woozy, and that to sit behind a steering-wheel at that moment was probably a little more than she could do in complete safety.

With very little fuss, Preston gave their wrist-keys to an attendant to collect their bags and asked him to meet them outside at the car. In a few moments Vanessa found herself sitting in the Porsche, huddled in yet another spare sweater which he dragged from his bag. She gritted her teeth purposefully so that she would stop shaking, and allowed the events of the day to bear her along on dreamy, unreal wings.

In keeping with the tone of the day, it began to rain and as the water swirled across the windscreen she tried to erase the image that still kept flashing in her mind of the two girls sinking beneath the water.

'Soon be in the warm,' the solid voice said beside her and she managed a smile.

Ten minutes later she found herself staring up at an

elegant terraced Georgian house built in a crescent amongst green trees, its long case windows being attacked by violent bursts of wind and rain which twisted the early leaves from the branches and whipped them into the air and across the pale brick.

'Come on,' he grinned, leaning across to push open her door. 'Let's put some colour back into those pale cheeks.'

On jelly-like legs she followed him up four white stone steps, and took her first glance into the domestic world of Dr Preston Lynley.

Had Tara come here? That was her first thought.

She knew that specialists often saw patients in their private rooms, sometimes at their own houses. This high-ceilinged, colourful house, with its bold blue and red rooms and its original Georgian windows with their accompanying sheath-like drapes, should have been rather a cold house to judge by its impressive and aloof exterior. But it wasn't. It was warm and welcoming, and although there were very few feminine touches amongst the solid mahogany wood and polished antiques everywhere seemed sparkling and cared for.

'Just leave your things in the room on the right,' he told her, and she wandered in, slowly absorbing the masculine comfort, the conker-brown leather chairs and a thick sprinkling of rugs on the polished floor. She gazed from one of the windows into the winding garden beyond. The rain had begun in earnest now.

She found her way back to the kitchen, which looked disturbingly space-age with all its gadgets and computerised controls. Preston had already begun tossing a salad, and grinned at her surprise.

'Coming home to operate a microwave,' he chuckled, 'is far easier than having to think for oneself.'

Vanessa gazed admiringly around her. 'So I see.'

'You don't approve?' he teased her.

She perched on a stool and cupped her chin thoughtfully

in her hands. 'On the contrary. This is heaven. I don't often cook unless I'm in the mood.'

He raised two dark, wry brows as he cracked eggs into the mixer. 'Which explains the diet of sardines on toast?'

She laughed, brushing back her tousled copper-coloured hair. 'I know it's no excuse, but I did more than the lion's share of cooking when I was living at home. Not that I minded, really. Mum died when we were ten and other than live off cans and crisps for the rest of our lives I decided to learn how to cook.' She realised, almost without thinking, that she had begun to reveal herself to him.

His face softened. 'That was very young to lose a parent.'

She nodded. 'Dad took it pretty badly. He tried to lose himself in his work, which left my sister and me to our own devices a lot of the time. It wasn't too bad, I suppose. Our friends often envied us our freedom, but I was the elder twin by twenty minutes and I always felt so responsible. . .I was trying to take the place of Mum, I suppose, determined to keep the family together.'

Preston watched her thoughtfully. 'And your father and sister still live in Brideport?'

Vanessa shook her head. 'Dad remarried when we started nursing and now lives with Jean in Canada. I lost my sister two years ago in an accident.'

His face was full of concern, but wisely he asked no questions. Instead he said simply, 'Then you've had a great deal of loss to handle. I'm sorry, Vanessa.'

She watched him turn to the hob and make the omelette very competently. She rummaged around in the drawers and laid the breakfast bar with knives and forks. Then they sat and devoured eggs, garnished with parsley and lightly buttered toast, and drank heaps of freshly squeezed orange juice.

'Tell me, where did you learn to swim like a fish?' He removed their plates and filled the dishwasher, and her eyes found his soft brown nape and the strong, round muscle of his shoulder as he bent down.

'At school. I was a natural in the water, but my sister couldn't bear it. Horses were the love of her life.'

He closed the dishwasher door and came to sit beside her, resting muscled brown forearms swirling with dark hair on the breakfast bar. 'We kept horses when I was a child. Kieron, my elder brother, and I were born in Scotland but my parents moved to the Midlands. We boarded, though, and rather lost contact with having animals.'

'Are your parents still in the Midlands?'

He looked askance. 'Heavens, no. They live in Greece. My father's retired from business and he bought some land out there some years ago. Unfortunately, the family rarely meet—Kieron lives in Sante Fe with his wife and two boys. He and Gabby have a ranch. It's a beautiful place. Mountains and green fields, like Scotland. I suppose, in a way, he's managed to get back to his roots.'

'Which was why you went out there?' she asked curiously. 'Looking for roots too?'

He paused, then shrugged. 'Who knows? Aren't we all trying to find ourselves in one way or another? But I think the overriding draw was the professional interest in sports medicine, for which there's an enormous call—much more so than in Britain.'

Vanessa felt her heart sink a little as the suggestion of sports medicine brought her back to the reason Tara had first consulted this man who had persuaded her into treatment that must have given her false hope to ride again.

It must have shown on her face because he suddenly looked concerned and arched a brow. 'Enough about me. Are you feeling any better?'

She nodded, chewing on her lip. 'Just a bit damp. I still have my swimsuit on. I think I'd better go home and have a shower.'

'Help yourself to one here, if you like. I've a few phone calls to make. Then I'll run you back to your car, if you feel up to it.' He began to clear the plates and she rose to help him. Then the phone rang and he picked up the extension which hung on the wall.

'Caroline. A query on a patient,' he mouthed. 'Take that shower, if you like. Upstairs, last on the left.'

She hesitated, then shrugged as he settled himself on a stool and flipped open his case on the worktop to pull out some papers.

She discovered the bathroom where Preston had indicated. A pile of thick white towels was stacked on a rack by a huge oval black bath. Long, elegant mirrors framed the walls and grey and white tiles led into an equally opulent, but indulgently masculine shower-room.

Before she showered she decided to find her sports bag. Peeping into each of the rooms, which were all large— and unoccupied—she satisfied her curiosity on the pretext of finding the bag. Finally she discovered it in what she supposed to be the master bedroom, a tasteful, discreet mixture of deep blues and greys—a thick, slate-grey carpet, austere white blinds and a bed which was bigger than hers and Charlie's put together.

Just to make sure that he was still on the phone, she listened at the top of the stairs and reassuringly heard his voice in the kitchen. Ten minutes was all it should take, she decided, and why not? Better than sitting and twiddling her thumbs waiting for him to finish.

Locking the door of the shower, she stripped swiftly and plunged gratefully under the hot jet of water. She borrowed a little shampoo and washed the chlorine out of her hair. When she had finished she felt much better and smothered herself in one of the warm white towels, then wrapped another around her head.

On the landing she heard no sound. Padding in bare feet to the bedroom, she relaxed. That was until a voice behind her said, 'I forgot, you'll need this.'

She spun around to find him holding a hairdryer. 'Oh, thanks,' she mumbled and blushed fiercely. At that moment the towel on her head seemed to unwrap itself and fell to the floor, freeing the long wet fronds of her hair to fall onto her naked shoulders.

'I'll get it,' he said and before she could move he had picked it up.

She realised later that it had been quite unnecessary for him to lay the dryer on the bed and to begin lifting her hair into the towel to try to rewrap it. But at the point where his fingers brushed her skin she seemed not to be thinking at all.

'You've beautiful hair,' he told her softly. 'And beautiful skin. Creamy and smooth against the deep red—'

'C-copper,' she corrected him lamely.

'Yes, I suppose it is. All those rich deep browns and golds. . .'

She felt the pull of his lungs under his ribcage as her breasts pushed against his chest when he moved to fiddle with the towel, and for a moment she held onto the reality which said that this could not be happening but almost in the same moment found the chemistry between them impossible to ignore. Reaching out to steady her swimming head, she gripped the taut, hard muscle of his arms as it moved under her fingertips.

'Vanessa,' he muttered huskily, making no attempt to release her as his arm slid around her waist. What happened next seemed inevitable, in a strange kind of way. Perhaps she had known it was going to happen; perhaps she had been expecting it to happen, she thought as a wave of heat washed over her.

'P-Preston, no,' she mumbled weakly.

'Do you want me to let you go?' His hand pressed a path along her spine and she gave a little gasp as he drew her closer. His eyes were shadowed and heavy, his lashes

fluttering gently against his cheeks like small dark butter-
flies against the grain of his skin.

'Vanessa,' he said again, and with a soft groan bent to
kiss her and she closed her eyes. Then she felt the soft
sensation of his hand slipping the towel away from her,
and his lips came down again on hers. Her mouth parted
for him and she stopped fighting, sliding her hands around
his neck.

He eased her down gently and she went, her body melting in his arms as his kiss deepened and she felt his hands
begin to unwrap her as they lay on the bed. Suddenly the
green eyes locked with hers and something in them made
her start, abruptly become aware, and she reached out and
grabbed her towel. 'No,' she said and sat up on the bed,
pulling her towel around her.

He stared at her with reproachful eyes. 'Isn't this what
you wanted, Vanessa? Be honest for once. Aren't you as
attracted to me as I am to you?'

'I came up here for a shower,' she replied shakily, her
heart racing. 'Just a shower—'

'Are you sure?'

She wasn't. Because she had enjoyed every moment;
had wanted him; had forgotten how it felt to be held in
that way and touched, with genuine human warmth and
longing, and how wonderful it was to respond—to let
everything slip away from mind. . .

'What is it, Vanessa?' he asked her softly, his brow
creased. 'There's something I don't understand, something
you're not telling me. When are you going to drop that
impenetrable guard of yours?'

'Because I've just refused to go to bed with you?' she
gasped, pulling the towel a little tighter, as if it would
help her ward off the laser-like inspection of the green
eyes which invaded her.

He looked at her for a long while and then stood up,
frustration written clearly in the deep and jagged lines

etched across his face. He walked across the room and opened the door. 'You'd better get dressed,' he said roughly and walked out.

She sat stiffly, staring into space and feeling absurdly cheated. Or at least her body did. It was still aching for him, her bared flesh throbbing where he had touched her and brought her alive. How long had it been since she had allowed anyone close to her? How long had she wrapped herself in an inflexible cocoon from the outside world? Perhaps, she thought in dismay as she pulled her clothes from her bag, it had been so long that she couldn't remember how she should respond to human affection.

One half-hearted attempt at falling in love with a medical student in her training years and several failed relationships afterwards which hadn't even got off the ground because she'd made excuses, always travelling back home in a panic in response to a distress call from Dad or Tara. . .that wasn't exactly a blueprint for success as far as relationships were concerned!

Not that she had been able to help much, even when she'd arrived back in Brideport. Dad had always been in despair with Tara's moods and her unpredictable behaviour and the stream of odd boyfriends who'd turned up at the house without warning and stayed until someone had politely ejected the freeloading lodger.

Again Vanessa felt the pang of guilt for having left them but, at twenty-one, she had thought that Tara had needed some independence. . .and Dad had found Jean, who had had precious little privacy with Dad anyway with two girls still living at home.

Forcing her reluctant limbs into her own grey track suit, she folded the clothes Preston had loaned her on the bed and then made her way downstairs. He was waiting for her, his tall figure moving to the bottom of the stairs as she came down.

'Feeling like driving?' he asked her and she nodded.

'But I thought I might get a taxi,' she protested weakly, unable to meet his gaze, 'to save dragging you out in this weather.'

'It's not a problem.' He opened the front door, his voice biting roughly as he led her out into the rain.

As she sat in the car and watched the brown hands deftly move over the steering-wheel her lips were still tingling and her body ached for him, the need almost overwhelming her to make him stop the car and take her in his arms and kiss her as he had upstairs in his bedroom. If the truth were known, she had wanted to snuggle up in the huge double bed with his wonderful body alongside her, bringing her back to life from the eternity she seemed to have spent asleep.

CHAPTER FIVE

AS WEEKENDS went, the next one was pretty unimpressive.

Charlie had to work, so Vanessa occupied herself with spring-cleaning the flat. Illogically, she found herself looking forward to Monday morning rather more than she should have been.

When Preston greeted her between surgeries she found herself hoping that he might stop and talk for a few moments, but he rarely did. True, they were busy and the surgeries were packed, but he maintained the same friendly but distant air for the following days, without waylaying her once.

She couldn't understand herself. It was irrational after trying so hard to dislike him and discourage him that now she was wondering why she didn't have his attention. Then, one glorious day, when the sun streamed through the window, reflecting dazzlingly off the roof of the black Porsche—which, irritatingly, just happened to be parked outside—and when she was trying hard not to think how she wished she could hear just one disparaging remark from a patient about Preston Lynley, Val buzzed through on the intercom.

'I know you're not supposed to have your next patient for ten minutes, Vanessa, but I've a young lady who would like to see you if you can manage it? She's a temporary resident—not registered with us, but she says you know her. She's Tim Robson's girlfriend.'

Vanessa shook herself out of her mood, twitched the blinds to shut out the gleam of the car and tried to recall the pale young woman who had disappeared that day she had seen Tim. 'Yes, Val, I remember. Send her along if she's completed the necessary forms.'

Very soon her new patient appeared. She was no longer dressed in sweater and jeans, as she had been when Vanessa had seen her last, but now wore a loose dress and her long brown hair was scraped back into a knot. She had a sallow complexion and dark eyes, made even darker by the rings around them.

Vanessa glanced at the temporary notes. 'Hello,' she welcomed in a friendly voice, 'Francesca, isn't it?'

The girl nodded and took a seat. 'I'm not ill or anything,' she said hesitantly, 'but I just wondered if you could give me a blood pressure check. I need the Pill soon and I know I have to be checked. I don't live permanently in Brideport. I come from up north.'

'And you're under a GP's care at home?'

She nodded. 'I forgot to bring a prescription with me.'

Vanessa began to unwrap the arm cuff of the meter, and pushed away the excess sleeve that seemed to fall around the girl's arm. She was shocked to find, as she did so, how thin the girl was and that the arm she was wrapping was no more than skin and bone. Trying not to reveal her dismay and checking the top and bottom figures on the sphygmomanometer, Vanessa found that she had a poor reading of low blood pressure.

'I'm usually a hundred and ten over seventy five,' the girl said sharply, aware of Vanessa's concentrated frown.

Vanessa was just about to answer when, to her surprise, Francesca looked up and said more softly, 'Though I've had flu and I've been a bit constipated lately. As a matter of fact, I wondered if you could give me a laxative whilst I'm here?'

Vanessa rolled back the cuff and put the meter to one side. 'Francesca, with your lower reading and your request for the Pill, I think I would like the doctor to see you. If you prefer, we have a lady doctor—'

'No!' Her patient jumped up, seemingly agitated. 'I'm

going back up north soon. Can't you give me something till then?'

Vanessa sensed that something was very wrong. She hesitated before replying because she had the feeling that Francesca would disappear as she had done before and the problem would remain unresolved.

'Unfortunately, without your medical records—' she began tentatively.

'Oh, it doesn't matter!' The girl picked up her bag and hurried to the door.

'Francesca, please wait a moment!' Vanessa tried to catch the door before it banged in her face, but she was too late. When she opened it she just caught sight of her patient disappearing through Reception's outer doors.

Avoiding the curious glances of other patients, Vanessa retreated back into her room. She was very disturbed by what had just happened and deeply worried about the girl when, as she stood there thinking about what she could do, the phone rang. As she picked it up her eyes fell on the car park through the window.

'Vanessa,' said Preston, 'could I catch you at one? It's about the Searles, as a matter of fact.'

Vanessa saw the tip of Francesca's head disappear into a car. 'Yes, all right,' she agreed distractedly. 'I'll meet you in the staffroom—'

'No,' he interrupted abruptly, 'not there. It might be in use.'

She frowned at his comment but she was preoccupied with watching the old banger reverse and drive swiftly past her window. 'Oh, where, then?' she murmured, biting her lip pensively.

'I've a call to make at a local nursing home. There's the Grey Lady close by. We could have a sandwich and sit in the garden—catch a breath of fresh air, perhaps. When is your first patient this afternoon?' he asked when she paused.

'Oh. . .' she glanced at her diary. 'I've nothing until three, I suppose—'

'Fine, I'll have you back here well before then. Meet me at the car at one,' he concluded and hung up.

After he had rung off she sat back and caught her breath. Well, there was nothing she could do about Francesca. She would just have to hope that the girl had gone off in a temper and after some sensible thought would make an appointment with a doctor.

Faced with the prospect of seeing Preston, Vanessa felt a quiver of excitement tingle through her body. Recalling how she had felt when he had taken her in his arms and kissed her, half of her tried to suffocate the recollection and half encouraged it, which meant that she felt about as confused as she had ever done regarding their relationship!

Vanessa freshened up in the cloakroom and brushed her hair onto her shoulders until it gleamed. Smoothing on a fresh coat of tawny lipstick, she took a deep breath, tried to look reasonably composed and told herself that this was a working lunch and not a social outing.

She passed the staffroom on her way out and was surprised to see Caroline Grey and Mike Shelley in there, revealed by the blinds which they had neglected to draw. Automatically she stepped back. Mike looked very gloomy—even agitated, which was unusual for Mike. Caroline stood by the window, her dark head bent—almost as though she were crying. Obviously there had been friction between them.

Quickly Vanessa turned away and hurried down the back stairs. By the time she reached the Porsche Preston was in it, waiting.

'Hop in,' he called, leaning over and pushing the door open.

She climbed in, smiling at him as she clicked her safety belt.

'Sorry if I've dragged you away,' he said with an apologetic shrug. 'But I know you've taken a keen interest in the Searles and I thought you'd like to keep abreast of matters.'

'Has something happened, then?' she asked anxiously, forgetting about the scene between Caroline and Mike.

'No, but I've heard from Katie's consultant,' he sighed. 'Look, I'll explain everything when we're sitting down with a sandwich. I'm afraid I couldn't contemplate going through the day without something to eat, and I thought it might be a good opportunity for us to have a chat.'

She sat back, uncomfortably aware that she was beginning to feel quite at home in the luxury of the car. Was it the car? she wondered. Or was it just being with him? Something about his company, his conversation, the way she felt as if she had known him for years and not just months. . .?

They were soon at the Grey Lady, a thatched pub built on the banks of a stream which wound through the town to the sea. The garden was deserted for a June day, and they sat by the stream under an umbrella and ate prawn sandwiches and drank cream soda sprinkled with ice.

'What about your nursing home?' Vanessa realised that she was enjoying herself so much that she'd forgotten his call.

'On the way back. I'll only be a few moments. I offered to deliver a couple of prescriptions—their driver is off with a cold this week.' He took a bite of his sandwich with a satisfied sigh of appreciation. Her eyes watched the long brown throat move and swallow as the voracious mouth above crunched away enthusiastically.

He grinned, catching her glance, and she blushed as he trapped her gaze. 'Thanks for coming,' he said softly. 'I rather thought you might not.'

'I was hungry,' she smiled. 'I couldn't refuse a free lunch, now, could I?'

'For someone who's hungry you've a strange way of showing it.' He glanced down at her plate, still untouched, and she jumped, picking it up immediately.

'It's all right,' he chuckled. 'I'm convinced.'

Which, of course, he wasn't, she realised in a flush of embarrassment. She was unable to decide whether he was merely teasing her or making a fairly successful effort at making her feel thoroughly flustered.

'Do you know, I can almost hear that brain of yours ticking away—trying to work out why I dragged you from surgery?' he intoned, leaning forward and arching his dark brows.

She blushed again. 'Do you blame me?'

'Oh, absolutely not,' he said with disarming honesty. 'But I promise Charlie won't need the knuckle-dusters just yet.'

She frowned, staring at him curiously under her dark lashes. 'Charlie?'

'Or is it Charles?'

Suddenly the penny dropped. He believed she was sharing the flat with her boyfriend! Well, who was she to dissuade him from the assumption? In fact, 'Charles' could possibly be a distinct advantage now she thought about it. It meant that she had her own infallible system of protection.

'No, not Charles. . .' She crossed her fingers under the table, telling herself that she wasn't exactly lying. 'It's just Charlie.'

'Charlie,' he repeated, and she averted her gaze, dropping it to her glass as she sipped her drink.

'And so, what were you going to tell me about Katie?' She decided to change the subject quickly.

'Ah, yes. Katie.' He nodded slowly, his eyes roaming her face with a strange expression, and her heart lurched as she hoped he wasn't managing to read her mind again.

'Have you talked to Sonia yet?' she prompted.

He nodded. 'I visited them yesterday. John Dale, Katie's consultant, had explained that on the one hand Katie might not develop further symptoms. As I anticipated, they want to take a biopsy of the synovium which encloses the worst affected joint in her knee and that would give a clearer picture. On the other hand, however, if it is Still's the sooner they diagnose it the better and then they can map out treatment. Unfortunately, Sonia's balked at John's suggestion of a biopsy.'

Vanessa took a breath. 'But why?'

'Because she refuses to admit the child has anything more than a viral infection. She says she believes Katie has recovered from her troubles of the last year and she will get over this. My feeling is that to accept Katie's problem will force Sonia to re-evaluate what has happened to them. By confronting a serious illness, it recalls the trauma of the cancer with her husband and the implications of another serious disease within the family.'

'You mean, she couldn't handle Katie being unwell?'

'Well, put yourself in her place. You lose a husband and face an unknown, unquantified threat to your daughter. It's all happened within the space of two years. Emotionally you could still be needing to grieve properly if you hadn't come to terms with your first loss. A potential second one is totally unacceptable.'

'But the disease isn't fatal, is it?'

He shook his head. 'It's extremely rare but, over the years, the muscles of the affected limbs could become weaker. In a small proportion of cases inflammation of the joints leads to partial or crippling deformity or even blindness. This, of course, is looking at the worst scenario, but it must be considered.' Vanessa turned her eyes away. She needed no great stretch of imagination to understand Sonia's reaction to the prospect. 'Which is where you come in,' he added, and with a sinking heart she turned to stare at him.

'But how can I help if Katie's own consultant can't?'

He shrugged. 'Just talk to her for me. Now, I know your feelings on this. And I'm not asking you to sell Sonia the idea—'

'But you are, aren't you?' she cut in, feeling as though she had been tricked into coming out to lunch with him. 'And the answer's no, Preston. Sonia must decide for herself. She has all the facts. She's the child's mother and knows best.'

'But surely it's Katie we should be thinking of? Her welfare? Her future?' He leaned forward, his green eyes intense. 'Mark my words, Vanessa, if it is Still's the child will need all the help she can get. It isn't a question of burying our heads in the sand and hoping for the best. These are the nineties—we can do something. The sooner treatment begins the better—you know that, as a professional.'

'It's not fair,' she objected in dismay. 'You're using emotional blackmail!'

He shook his head, reaching out to take her arm. 'Rubbish. All I'm asking is that you help us persuade Sonia to let us take Katie in for the biopsy. At least it would be a start.'

'And what if she refuses?'

'Then I suppose we'll have to leave it at that.'

Vanessa tried to ignore her rising anger at being used, and yet in a strange way his theories as far as Sonia went seemed to strike a personal note somehow.

'I've an idea,' he suggested suddenly. 'Look over a couple of cases with me—I've several papers on case histories of Still's. See what you think.'

Vanessa looked up him and saw the enthusiasm burning brightly in his face, although he was doing a good job of trying to cover it. There was no doubt that he bore a deep concern for his patients. Here was a man not easily triumphed over by adversity, no matter in what form it appeared. She might not agree with his methods but, then, who was to say that her opinion was any more valid than his?

'I'll give it some thought,' she prevaricated, determined that she would not be railroaded into compliance, no matter how strongly he felt on the subject.

It was another ten days before the subject of Katie was resurrected.

Vanessa called at mid-week on the Searles, her conscience pricking her to the extent that she thought she might simply call in to see how Katie was. But Katie had gone back to school, 'feeling better', according to Sonia— who herself was bright and breezy and seemed convinced that the child had recovered.

Pleasantly surprised, Vanessa did not feel inclined to pursue the subject, thinking that the problem might be resolved and that, in fact, Katie might have a complete recovery. When she explained this to Preston and conveyed both her and Sonia's high hopes he said very little, clearly disappointed. But she had little time to fall out with him over it as she had organised an intensive Well Woman Special, on a 'drop in and be seen' basis, for five days.

The response was astonishing. Many women at work came in their lunch hours and Vanessa dispensed with hers completely, grabbing a sandwich whenever she could.

Mrs Lithgow attended and brought her friend, who had not had a breast check in twenty years. Pat Sanderson was just forty-two and, as she entered Vanessa's room, remarked immediately that she had only come because her friend, Mrs Lithgow, had persuaded her.

Vanessa tried to make her feel comfortable but, when Pat undressed and slipped off her bra, she could not contain her surprise when she unwrapped from a wad of cotton wool a large ganglion, growing just below the left breast.

'I don't want it removed,' Pat said as Vanessa began to examine her. 'I've had it all these years and it hasn't given me any trouble.'

Vanessa was on the brink of explaining that a small op at the surgery would save her trouble and anxiety and certainly a great deal of investment in cotton wool but Pat eyed her darkly and said that she was not prepared to discuss it.

Vanessa sighed inwardly but continued with her check of each breast, lifting both Pat's arms to examine the hollow beneath and then downward, carefully probing for any lumps or abnormalities. 'All's well,' she said at last. 'Shall we take a smear while you're here and a BP check?'

Pat Sanderson wrapped her ganglion in cotton wool again and replaced her bra. 'How long will it take?' she asked curtly.

'No more than fifteen minutes.' Vanessa smiled. 'You've had half of the Well Woman examination; it seems a pity not to have the other half—and all absolutely free of charge,' she joked.

Pat was distinctly reluctant, determined not to enjoy the conversation, but Vanessa managed to persuade her at last by showing interest in her extensive family and her first grandchild—a source of great enjoyment, she learned.

When the smear had been taken and Vanessa had a reading of blood pressure she managed to update Pat's notes by asking questions surreptitiously. Finally, Vanessa thanked her warmly for coming, and explained that she should ring for smear results in four to six weeks. Surprisingly, Pat seemed reluctant to go for a moment as she hesitated at the door.

'There's nothing else I can help you with, is there?' Vanessa asked gently.

'Well. . .not really. . .no.' Her patient shrugged and then went on her way. Vanessa stared after her, wishing that she could have done more to help and sensing that she could—if given the opportunity. Still, some you win, she thought on a sigh, and some you lose. Pat Sanderson, she suspected, was not a happy woman.

One day, after the completion of her Well Woman campaign, Francesca Jay appeared in Reception and asked to see her.

'I've decided to stay in Brideport a bit longer,' she explained, not looking particularly comfortable as she spoke softly so that the girls at Reception could not hear.

'Come in,' Vanessa said, indicating her empty room. 'I've no one for ten minutes.'

Francesca followed her and sank nervously onto the edge of a chair. 'Tim's going to let Dr Lynley have a look at his knee in hospital. . .and I thought. . .I might stay to see how he got on.'

'I'm glad,' Vanessa responded with a friendly smile. 'Now, how can I help you?'

'I'm sorry about last time.' The girl clenched her hands in her lap. Vanessa noticed how thin they were and how much thinner overall she seemed to be since her last visit. 'It's embarrassing. . .'

'The constipation problem?' Vanessa guessed.

'I. . .I think, well, you see, I think I've left it too long. I think I need an enema. Nurses give enemas don't they?'

Startled, Vanessa nodded. 'Yes, in some cases. What makes you think you need such a radical treatment, Francesca?'

The girl blushed heavily, made more noticeable by her sallow skin and the prominence of her cheek-bones as they jutted out of her face below the deep grey hollows of her eyes. 'It's just been a while since. . .well, you know.'

Vanessa paused, her mind going over the facts she knew and the facts she obviously did not know about her patient. One thing was glaringly obvious. The girl, even though she was dressed once again in a baggy sweater and jeans, was painfully thin, possibly anorexic. Before they went any further there was a step she must take. She got up from her desk and walked to the weighing machine. 'Francesca, if you'd just like to hop on here?'

Her thin face contorted and she stared at the machine.

'This is just to record your weight, nothing more.'

'No, no,' she protested and held her head in her hands. 'I. . .I shouldn't have come.' And before Vanessa could reach her she had turned a deathly white and swayed in the chair. Vanessa just managed to break her fall as she tumbled to the floor.

'Lord, what's going on?' Preston muttered as he appeared from out of nowhere, rushing in to kneel beside them.

'I had just suggested that I weigh her, which she refused, and was terribly upset,' Vanessa explained in dismay. 'Preston, I think she's anorexic.'

He nodded slowly. 'It's Francesca Jay, isn't it?'

Vanessa said it was just as the girl stirred, and they helped her slowly into a sitting position. When her eyes fluttered open they lifted her between them to a chair.

'Now, what's all this about?' Preston's voice was gentle, but his tone was firm. 'Why do you think you fainted, Francesca?'

She shook her head, her long hair falling limply over her face.

'Have you eaten this morning?' He glanced at Vanessa, who shrugged.

'What have you eaten today?' he repeated again.

She hesitated, holding her thin hand to her mouth. 'Toast. . .I think.'

'And how long ago was that?'

She shook her head, keeping her face hidden under her hair. 'I. . .can't remember.'

Preston stood upright and looked at Vanessa. 'A glass of water, I think, is called for. Will you be all right for a moment while we fetch some, Francesca?'

He raised his brows and Vanessa knew very well that she could pour a glass from the tap in the treatment room, but that he wanted to speak to her out of Francesca's hearing.

'There's nothing to her body weight,' he said in the corridor after quietly closing the door behind them. 'When I helped her up I felt merely bone. She's a skeleton. No wonder she was agitated when you wanted to weigh her.'

Vanessa nodded. 'This is the second time she has approached me for laxatives, and this morning she was actually asking for an enema.'

His face darkened. 'I'll talk to her but, without notes, I'm at a disadvantage before I begin. She might be receiving treatment already, and I'll have to try to ascertain if she's on any medication. Chances are, she'll deny being underweight and she'll refuse to be treated.'

'But she's obviously ill,' Vanessa gasped. 'Isn't there anything we can do?'

He thought for a moment, then said, 'I'll need to use your phone. If I can't get any sense out of her I won't be happy to let her go. I think she needs hospitalisation and assessment. Brideport General has a special unit, fortunately. If they've a spare bed I might be able to get her in if I can convince her she needs help.'

She nodded. 'Can I help in any way?'

'I need her medical history—and I need to know who her GP is. Try contacting Tim for me. He might be able to shed a little light on it.'

Vanessa nodded, biting on her lip. 'I shouldn't have let her go last time,' she sighed worriedly.

He touched her arm. 'If she was determined to hide her anorexia there was nothing you could have done. Besides which, she may have some other medical problem we don't know about.'

Vanessa moved away and then remembered that he had

come looking for her. 'I'm sorry, did you want me for something?'

He shrugged. 'It can wait. I've a visit to make later. Katie Searle.'

Vanessa bit her lip, wondering what was coming next, but he smiled and gave her a little push. 'Go and have a bite to eat yourself. I'll take care of Francesca. We'll talk later. Oh, if you can reach Tim on the phone let me know, will you?'

A request with which she would have liked to comply, but on the number she had for Tim there was no reply and, other than physically going to knock at his door— which she couldn't manage because she had patients to see—there was little else she could do.

With five minutes to spare before her next Well Woman patient, she went to the staffroom and made herself a coffee, taking a deep breath as she collected her thoughts. It was a large, spacious, smokeless zone and the summer breeze fluttered in through the vertical blinds.

She realised as she sat there that once again Preston had been there when she'd needed him. And, if she was honest, she knew that he was a first-class doctor—which was so at variance with the mental picture she'd had of the man who had so damningly precipitated Tara into useless private treatment.

She closed her eyes and tried to think of an explanation. But she couldn't. She was even beginning to forget Tara's face, so instilled into her mind once that she'd known every expression, every nuance, that had ever passed over it.

Surprisingly, Francesca Jay put up no resistance to being admitted an hour later to Brideport General. Vanessa didn't have time to see Preston, but in the later part of the afternoon he caught her in Reception and told her what had happened.

He had just spoken on the phone to Tim, who had

returned from a hospital physio appointment. The bomb-shell was that he had very little idea of his girlfriend's background. She had always been very secretive of her past and he didn't know of her doctor, or even where she lived in the north.

'But didn't he notice her weight?' Vanessa asked in surprise.

Preston shrugged. 'He's preoccupied with his own knee troubles at the moment. And Francesca told him she was doing some modelling which took her all over the country, and this seemed to cover any queries he had.' He raised his eyebrows. 'It's rather a tempestuous relationship, as far as I can gather. I'll let you know as soon as I hear from the hospital. Meanwhile, I'll get on to the Family Practitioners' Committee and see if they can help trace records for me.'

That night, although she could not pass on details of the case to Charlie, Vanessa explained how disturbed she had been to see a young patient with such advanced anorexia.

Charlie said something strange, and it played on Vanessa's mind later as she tried to sleep. She had said that she had read a book once which suggested that anor-exia was a form of control, in so far as not eating could mean that a person could reinvent themselves through con-tinual starving.

Vanessa had nodded vaguely, deep in her own thoughts, wishing she had been able to spot Francesca's problem the first time. After all, the girl was so thin. But, then, Tara had been thin and yet so full of energy and life. She finally fell asleep, but even when she woke in the morning she was still thinking about what Charlie had said.

Later that day Preston told her that he had visited Katie and she was unwell again, with a temperature of 39.5°C.

Vanessa sighed, intensely disappointed. 'Will Sonia agree to the biopsy?'

He shook his head. 'She's still adamant.'

Vanessa thought about it for the rest of the day and then went to Preston later that afternoon. She found him in his room, concentrating on notes propped on his desk— several sheets of which were spread in front of him—and he looked up with a frown.

'Busy?' she asked.

'No, not particularly. Come in.'

She walked slowly to his desk and saw that the papers were Katie's and that the expression on his face was one of frustration. 'If you're not on call this evening,' she suggested on the spur of the moment, 'would you care to run over Still's disease with me?'

He leaned back in his chair and the frown vanished as he rolled his eyes exultantly. 'That's music to my ears, Nurse Perry. At my place or yours?'

Vanessa shrugged. 'I thought here.'

'Aagh!' he groaned, dropping his head into his hands. 'Much too much like hard work. Come to my place—and bring your Charlie with you. It's about time we met, I think, don't you?'

She had landed herself in a mess and she knew it.

Why, in heaven's name, hadn't she told him the truth about Charlie? Vanessa stared in the mirror that evening and considered her reflection. Blue jeans on her long legs, pale grey tie-waist shirt catching the grey, uncertain flame in her eyes, and her hair a coppery halo around her head, spinning out in molten tendrils around her face.

But it was beside the point what she looked like! She couldn't take Charlie to Preston's house because Charlie was a girl and she was out with Ken, anyway.

Vanessa sighed and for a moment curled up beside the phone, pondering her predicament. Then she dialled and listened, heart in mouth.

'Preston, I've changed my mind,' she said quickly

before her courage deserted her, 'I'm sorry if I'm letting you down at the last moment, but—'

'You're going to tell me Charlie can't make it. Guys' night out—something like that? And you don't want to come without him?'

'Well. . .er. . .I'm not sure I would put it like that—'

'No problem. I'll come to you.'

'I thought perhaps we could leave it until another evening,' she suggested meekly.

'It's no trouble. I've a pretty good stack of textbooks and I've several case papers I've sorted out, too. I'll leave them with you to browse through, if you like.'

She mumbled away like a fool and then finally gave in. When she replaced the phone she felt a heel and when he arrived, balancing textbooks and papers in a stack in front of him so that only his eyes twinkled above them, she felt even more guilty—all because she had allowed a misunderstanding to develop over Charlie's name.

'Do you. . .do you want to come up?' she asked as she greeted him at the front door.

'Feel safer on home territory?' he grinned.

'Should I worry about being safe?'

He chuckled. 'My hands are tied,' he said and jiggled the pile. She avoided his green gaze and muttered something inaudible. He followed her up the two flights of stairs into the flat, carefully lowering the books onto the dining table—where they overbalanced and he rearranged them in smaller piles. Then, delving into the middle pile, he tugged out a folder and waggled it in front of her nose. 'Case histories. Two girls. One six, the other eight.'

Vanessa took them. 'Why girls?'

'Because girls are affected about twice as often as boys.'

'A fact?'

'Absolutely. Want to know more?' He began to pull off his sweater and before Vanessa could answer she found herself trying not to stare at the broad chest under a white

T-shirt, and long, muscled brown arms that flexed as he pulled a chair to sit at the table.

'Symptoms,' he said, and spread out the pages of a book with firm fingers. 'And Katie, like this girl of six, has all the classic symptoms.'

She sat on a chair beside him, her leg bumping the pair beside her clad in muscle-hugging jeans.

'Eyes,' he said and pointed to the text he had underlined. 'We know that sometimes inflammation of the eyes can lead to partial or complete blindness, and Katie has been complaining of soreness of her eyes since the beginning of the year. Joints. We know the sites of inflammation vary considerably from child to child. So far, it's Katie's legs—just as we have here. She says they are aching and have been increasingly problematic since as far back as last year.'

Vanessa nodded. 'They are incredibly alike.'

'Research shows that diet may be an important factor,' he explained, opening yet another vast tome in front of them. 'A nutritious, high-protein diet is recommended in cases of Still's, plus intensive physio and corticosteroid drugs—which might be necessary at first, but certainly not for long-term treatment with a child. This girl was introduced to a diet regime at six and responded well over the next twenty-four months. By the time she was twelve the disease was in check and by fifteen she was leading a normal adolescent life, but still maintaining her diet.'

Vanessa shifted her position slightly as his arm brushed her. 'And. . .er. . .the anaemia?' she managed, blinking at the text as his arm brushed her skin again and she could have sworn she felt a snap of electricity!

'At the worst a transfusion, but at the moment I've started her on a course of iron injections and, with luck, her new eating regime would improve her anaemia in the long term, just as we see here.'

'And what about Sonia?' Vanessa asked doubtfully.

He paused, his eyes thoughtful. Her gaze was distracted by their intensity and the curved half-moons of thick black lashes sweeping down over them. 'Well, I've endeavoured to explain, without seeming too concerned or making too light of it. I don't want to alarm her but at the same time we'll need her co-operation with the physio when she'll have to help Katie with the schedule of exercises.'

Vanessa nodded and sat back with a sigh. 'Perhaps we had better go over the case histories thoroughly first.'

As he talked she tried hard to concentrate on all the details. If she saw Sonia she would need to know all she could about the disease, and even if she did persuade Sonia to let Katie have a biopsy what would the woman's reaction be if Still's was confirmed?

Deciding that she would take one hurdle at a time, she began to lose herself in the gentle drone of his voice as he talked and it seemed only a few minutes later when she looked up to see that it was dark outside and that the lamp needed to be switched on in the room. He stretched his long arms as she did so and straightened his back against the chair.

'Coffee?' she offered and, at his nod, went to make it. When she came back with two mugs he was standing by the dresser holding a photo of Charlie in his hands and she almost dropped the coffee.

'Who's this?' he asked, replacing the photo.

'Someone from training days,' she managed, and held out the mug which he took with a curious smile. Then he lifted a brow and glanced at the easy chair, which was stacked with magazines, and the sofa. Since the sofa was the only decent piece of furniture on which to sit, apart from the hard wooden dining chairs, she gestured to it. 'Try the sofa. It's quite comfy.'

He moved to it and sank down into its battered but comfortable cushions. Then with a faint smile he asked, 'And where is Charlie tonight?'

Vanessa gulped her hot coffee. 'Oh, with a friend.'

'Aha!' He stared at her with amused eyes.

'A male friend,' she clarified, and then felt like kicking herself, for how long could she possibly go on with this absurd deception? She made up her mind to tell him, pulled back her shoulders—deciding that she could do it better on two feet—and promptly tripped over the rug, sending her coffee flying through the air.

She saw him wince as the hot liquid flew across the white T-shirt and burgeoned like a map of the world in front of her eyes. Before she realised what she was doing she was pulling at the steaming cloth, her fingers trembling as she tugged it away from his skin and over his head. Then she forced him to put up his arms up and snatched the whole thing off, her breath catching in her throat as she saw the imprint of the spill on his chest, not quite disguised by the thick forest of dark hair which spiralled over the taut brown muscles.

'Well, if this is the way to get your attention, give me scalding hot coffee any day,' he laughed as she stared in horror.

'But I've scalded you!'

He winced dramatically. 'Indeed you have. I think I'm going to need treatment of rather an intensive kind.'

'Don't joke!' she protested and ran to the bathroom to soak a towel with cold water. Coming back, she knelt on the sofa beside him and pressed the wet cloth gently over his chest. 'Is that better?' she whispered, feeling the heat burn through the towel to the palm of her hands.

'Mmm,' he sighed, his green eyes closing. 'Why ever didn't I think of having an accident before?' He lifted the edge of the cloth and scrutinised the inflamed skin beneath then, tossing it aside, he drew her down into his arms and pressed his mouth firmly over hers.

Several mind-shattering seconds later she was still in

his arms, and very much about to kiss him back, when the door opened and Charlie stood there, her eyes almost popping out of her head.

CHAPTER SIX

VANESSA'S lips were still throbbing as she tried to arrange her thoughts into some kind of sentence which would make the whole embarrassing scenario disappear. . .something like Abracadabra. . .but there wasn't a whisker of a hope of a miracle, or of the earth opening up under her feet and conveniently swallowing her as Charlie managed— eventually—to close her mouth.

Preston let her go and she jumped up, tugging down her rumpled shirt. He stood up beside her, frowning at Charlie, and Vanessa swallowed and knew there was nothing else to do but introduce them.

'Preston. . .' she began half-heartedly, 'this is. . .a friend of mine, er. . . Charlotte Wentworth.'

Charlie frowned at Vanessa fleetingly, then beamed a radiant smile at their guest. 'But it's Charlie to everyone on Planet Earth,' she laughed easily.

In retrospect, Vanessa was forced to admit that he took it pretty well. He smiled and held out his hand, a small muscle working in the base of his jaw as he replied. Eventually, he collected his sweater and pulled it on over his bare chest. 'It's been a pleasure to meet you, Charlie,' he said politely, 'but I'm afraid I must go.'

'Oh, please don't leave on my account.'

'I don't want to outwear my welcome,' he told her, flicking a dark glance in Vanessa's direction. They watched him gather his books and stride to the door. Vanessa, still rooted to the spot, closed her eyes. When she opened them he was staring at her. The smile had evaporated from his lips and his cold green gaze said what words could not.

How could she have done it? How could she have let him discover her lying like that? She didn't even try to follow him down the stairs. What could she say? How could she explain her deception and how it had all started off so innocently? It suddenly mattered terribly that he knew the truth. He was the one person in the world she did not wish to think badly of her.

Charlie stared at her in wonderment. 'Vanessa, are you crazy? He's gorgeous. And I've been thinking, after the picture you've painted, he would turn out to be like a double helping of Crippen!'

'You don't understand, Charlie.' Vanessa slumped down into a chair, holding her head in her hands. 'I've made such a mess of things.'

'I would say you were doing pretty well until I came in and spoiled it for you.'

Vanessa looked up, her huge grey eyes like watery moons and her coppery hair tousled in abandon around her face as she slid her fingers achingly through it. 'It wasn't like that. . .at least, not what it seemed.'

Charlie sighed. 'I just wished I'd stayed out for another couple of hours, that's all, but Ken started a migraine and I came home early.'

'Oh, it doesn't matter.' Vanessa shook her head. 'I would have had to tell him about you some time or other.'

'Me?' Charlie gaped at her. 'Where do I fit into the scheme of things?'

Vanessa chewed her lip, preparing herself for Charlie's reaction. 'I've not been entirely truthful, you see. I allowed him to think I lived here with a flatmate called Charlie.'

Charlie shrugged. 'Well, it's true, isn't it?'

'Yes, in a way. But he assumed Charlie was a man and. . .'

'And you didn't bother to correct him!' Charlie gasped.

'But for how long did you think you could keep the truth hidden?'

Vanessa sighed deeply. 'Oh, I don't know. At first it all seemed to fit rather well and then it got out of hand. When he asked us to visit his house tonight I had to refuse and then he came here—and then you walked in.'

'And turned out to be a woman,' Charlie groaned. 'Do you think he was upset with you?'

Vanessa bit her lip. 'Just imagine if Ken had played that kind of dirty trick on you. What would you think?'

'I'd think he was a swine!'

'Exactly.'

Charlie paused, furrowing her brow. 'Have you asked him about Tara yet?'

Vanessa shook her head. 'I haven't had the chance.'

'Or have you deliberately avoided it?' suggested Charlie relentlessly. 'Because you're afraid of an answer you don't want to hear?'

Was she really afraid to ask him? she wondered as she stared at Charlie wordlessly. Afraid of facing the fact that she hadn't known Tara as well as she'd thought? She tried to shut out the picture of Preston's expression tonight as it suddenly sprang to life in front of her eyes, his eyes full of reproach.

Later, unable to sleep, she sat up in bed and switched on the bedside light. With a lump in her throat she decided that sooner or later she'd have to confront Preston about Tara—though she couldn't blame him if he chose to ignore her for the remainder of her time at the practice.

But she was in for a surprise.

Not only did he speak to her in a reasonably civilised manner—which perversely made her feel even more miserable—he called her in to assist with a patient, Liam Kettering, a soldier who had been injured in a bomb blast in Belfast.

The young man, a temporary resident who was staying with his mother in Brideport, had been partially blinded three months previously. 'My specialist in Ireland told me that with time my eyesight would improve,' he explained. 'They took a hammering but aren't irreparably damaged. My left one's worse as the explosion harmed part of the optic nerve.'

Preston put on gloves, as did Vanessa. He began to examine Liam's eyes, studying the left carefully with an ophthalmoscope, eventually passing the device to Vanessa.

'My CO's having my medical history faxed on to a mainland GP,' Liam went on. 'As I'm convalescing with Mum I wonder if I could give you as my doctor?'

Preston nodded as he gently examined the swollen lids. 'By all means. As far as I can see, your eyes obviously need to be swabbed and irrigated frequently. Nurse Perry here will be carrying out your treatment.' Preston glanced swiftly at her. Her heart lurched as she hoped to read warmth in it, some kind of intimacy which would make her feel better. But there was nothing but the brief, polite professionalism that she would have expected from a doctor regarding his nurse.

'Hi,' said Liam, unaware of her thoughts as he talked of the relatively small but vicious explosion which he barely remembered but which had arrested his career in the forces. 'I gave my service address to one of the girls and my CO's name. Is there anything else you want to know?'

Preston pulled off the gloves and rinsed his hands. 'I think it best I contact your CO personally. As soon as I have medical details we'll be able to start you on treatment. Meanwhile, I'll leave you in the capable hands of Nurse Perry for a straightforward irrigation with saline.'

'Thanks, Dr Lynley.' The young man blinked painfully and Vanessa settled him back and drew a waterproof cape around him, casting a last look in Preston's direction before he left the room. However, he didn't return her glance and closed the door, leaving her to tackle the irrigation.

The washing-out of the soldier's eyes absorbed her concentration and she was thankful of it as she swabbed and cleaned very gently. However, Liam's colourful and humorous tales of army life still didn't prevent her mind from returning to Preston and the distant manner in which he had treated her.

'See you soon, and thanks, Nurse Perry.' Eventually Liam slipped on his dark glasses and went to Reception to make his next appointment. She was tempted to follow as she heard Preston's voice in Reception saying that he wanted to see Liam the following day. And then she decided against it. If Preston wanted to talk to her he knew where to find her. After his cool politeness that morning, she hadn't the heart to attempt any more conversation. At lunchtime, though, she found herself idling in the staff room hoping that he might come in. He didn't. At five, when she walked out, the Porsche was gone.

Charlie was unhelpfully blunt that night. 'He's only doing what you wanted him to do,' she sighed with doom-laden enthusiasm. 'Keeping from pestering you. He probably knows you feel embarrassed and is doing the gentlemanly thing in avoiding you for a bit.'

'I felt a lemon today, sitting alone in the staffroom,' Vanessa admitted. 'I hoped he might just look in, but he didn't.'

'Well, what can you expect?' Charlie philosophised. 'First you accuse him, then you put him on trial...then you let him believe—'

Vanessa didn't wait to hear the end of Charlie's home truths and called over her shoulder that she was going to make a drink. After making it and delivering a steaming mug of hot chocolate to Charlie, who was now glued to

TV, she took a long, foamy soak in the bath and decided on an early night.

She was beginning to lose count of the nights she was going to bed before ten! On this particular night it was to find lying on her bed the case history of the six-year-old she had discussed with Preston. Realising that he had left it behind and that Charlie had probably put it there for her to return, she browsed through the pages once more as she sat in bed, thinking of Katie and her mother.

Sonia had lost her husband and was in danger of losing a grip on Katie's health. She must be terrified inside, just as she herself had been when Tara had died and Dad had emigrated to Canada. Vanessa reread the case history and then flicked off her light. If she could not help herself or resolve the confusion she felt over Preston she at least knew now what she was going to do about Sonia and Katie Searle.

When Sonia Searle opened the door next day her face had aged ten years. She was without make-up and her hair straggled around her face. She invited Vanessa into Katie's bedroom but without enthusiasm. As Katie lay in bed in a light doze Vanessa tiptoed back out and whispered to Sonia.

'I shan't disturb her, but I'd love a cup of tea if you'll have one with me?'

Sonia nodded and together they went downstairs to the kitchen. Vanessa sat down at the kitchen table and they sipped tea.

'I expect she'll be back at school next week,' Sonia said eventually, stirring her tea aimlessly around in her cup.

'Sonia, let me help.' Vanessa held the older woman's eyes as she looked up. 'I lost my mother when I was ten and my twin sister two years ago. I understand how you're feeling and I really would like to help if I can.'

And then, as if the words had been the key which

unlocked the door of grief for Sonia Searle, the tears flowed and Vanessa shuffled her chair beside her and held her hand as she listened to the deep sobs as Sonia began to talk over the months she had spent nursing her husband through his illness and the final weeks he had spent in the hospice before his death.

Much later Vanessa left the house and went home to Chandler's Row, exhausted and spent but feeling strangely calm and at peace. Charlie was not there so she sat in silence, with yet another cup of tea, letting the peacefulness wash over her.

The following day was Friday and though she did not see Preston there was a note on her desk when she went in.

'Sonia rang me last night. Biopsy's on. Preston.'

Vanessa stared at it and reread it. It was encouraging news on the Searles, but the note itself was so impersonal that she felt hopelessly disappointed.

At lunchtime she made up her mind to see him and went along to his room, but at her knock there was no response. Just then Val tapped her on the shoulder.

'Looking for Preston, Vanessa?'

'Has he gone on visits?'

'Of a kind,' she chuckled softly. 'Didn't you know? He flew to Greece this morning.' Val stared at her curiously as Vanessa's face registered surprise. 'Weren't you at the practice meeting?'

Again Vanessa shook her head. 'I've been a bit. . .er. . . busy. I didn't think the meeting was terribly important.'

'Oh, it isn't usually,' Val admitted ruefully. 'Mostly the organisation is left to Beth, who does things in her own sweet way and the formalities are just observed at meetings. But this time it happened that Preston put in for an unscheduled week's leave. His father isn't very well, I believe.'

Vanessa tried not to sound too disappointed. 'Nothing serious, I hope?'

'Not that I know of. Is there anything I can help you with?'

'Nothing that can't wait.' Vanessa hesitated. 'When do you expect him back?'

'A week Monday, if all goes to plan. We've a locum coming to help us out in the meantime.' Val hurried off as someone called from Reception, and Vanessa walked to her room and sat down. He hadn't told her—or rung—and yet he must have known that he was going. Yet why should he after what had happened? In all probability, he hadn't given her a thought!

She determined to enjoy the week, with the good news of Sonia to help her along. That, at least, contributed to restoring her spirits even if Preston hadn't gone overboard in the note. After all, it was a glorious July and who could be miserable with such perfect weather? The countryside was beautiful, the evenings were long and Ken and Charlie had asked her to go to a barbecue with them at the weekend. Casting her eyes determinedly to her list, she saw that Liam was first to be seen.

'Dr Lynley has started me off on special treatment,' Liam told her when he came in. 'It's all on the computer now, apparently.'

Vanessa lifted her brows. Preston hadn't called her in to discuss Liam's treatment—and it was important. He had gone dashing off to wherever it was, but five minutes to help her to review the case wouldn't have gone amiss. 'I see Dr Lynley wants saline irrigation, swabbing with a special prescription he has left for you and gentamicin drops to both your eyes,' she murmured thoughtfully.

'He said to tell you he'd left the cream in the dispensary,' Liam told her, settling back in the chair. 'It's all labelled up.'

'He did, did he?' Vanessa felt a pang of annoyance.

'He did my treatment for me yesterday.' Liam tucked the plastic cape around himself. 'He said he didn't like to bother you, so would I pass it on?'

Vanessa took a breath. 'Well, thank you. But it would have been no trouble to have popped in, Liam. That's what I'm here for. Even if I was with another patient I wouldn't have kept you long. And perhaps you can mention that to Dr Lynley, should the need ever arise again. But, hopefully, you're my patient now and I have all the relevant details here on computer.'

'It's nice being spoiled,' laughed Liam. 'In the services you're lucky if you get an old dragon of a nur—'

Vanessa laughed softly as the boy stopped and went scarlet. 'I expect you lads need to be kept firmly in check,' she reproved gently, 'and a younger, less experienced nurse might have her work cut out, don't you think?'

'Too right,' her patient agreed enthusiastically. 'But you're young and you manage.'

'I'm not surrounded by a platoon of men, am I? I might be lost for words then!' she smiled, smoothing on her gloves and beginning the irrigation, although she thought a platoon of men might be a lot easier to handle than one particular man at this moment in her life.

Thanks to the weather, the barbecue was rained off on Saturday night.

Ken and Charlie disappeared on the Sunday in the little orange Beetle to a Beetle rally, leaving Ken's BMW parked outside the flat to remind Vanessa of the long day ahead of her.

On Monday she woke up with hay fever and, despite a course of antihistamine from the newly arrived locum, sneezed herself through three of the next four days.

When Friday arrived she felt worn out and listless and tried a swim at Centresport, but she kept thinking of the harrowing moments of the near-drowning. Leaving the pool, she opted for the sauna but the warmth merely brought on a reflective mood and she found herself pondering Caroline Grey and wondering how deeply she was involved with Preston. Eventually she left Centresport, having totally exhausted her body but lubricated her mind in just the way she had tried to avoid.

On Sunday she cooked a lunch for Charlie, who was off duty, and they went for a drink at the local with Ken in the evening. But Vanessa felt a gooseberry and left early, pleading a headache.

The next morning she found herself taking just that extra bit of care with her appearance. She washed her hair until it shone and spun lustrously out over her shoulders. She wore a new deep blue uniform she'd been saving for a rainy day, brand new smoky black stockings and dainty new black, low heeled shoes.

Charlie embarrassed her with a wry remark about Preston's return but she denied her anticipatory flush as new blusher and forced herself to drive very slowly, her heart leaping with excitement when she saw the Porsche and not the locum's old Ford parked in its familiar place beneath her window.

When she entered Reception she called a good morning to the girls and went straight to her room. Her heart followed the same crazy course as it had in the car park when she saw the note on her desk.

'Can you spare a few minutes? P,' it said briefly.

Perhaps, if she hadn't felt like a seventeen-year-old with a flush raging up to her cheeks and her pulse drumming in her ears like a symphony orchestra, she might have sensed or even heard something before she pushed open Preston's door. But for the second time she came abruptly to a halt as on this occasion she disturbed Caroline Grey completely wrapped in Preston's arms. He had a look on his face which was totally concentrated on Caroline and which made Vanessa feel as though the bottom of her world had suddenly fallen out.

Preston took a few seconds to make eye contact. By which time Vanessa had spun around, a pain darting across her ribs as tears of embarrassment and bewilderment filled her eyes before she managed to reach the safety of her room and grab a handful of tissues.

At least Caroline hadn't seen her. At least she hadn't been made to look a fool twice in the space of a few weeks, she told herself. At least now she knew for certain what was going on, though she would have given anything not to have walked in on them again—as though once wasn't enough!

The problem now, she realised, was to keep up a façade, which was going to be difficult as they worked together.

Luckily, she was occupied with a wound redressing when Val phoned her and asked if she was free to see Dr Lynley.

'Sorry, Val,' Vanessa said. 'I'm still with Mrs Grainger and I'm a little behind this morning.'

'Don't worry,' Val answered. 'Catch you later.'

'Busy morning,' said Mrs Grainger as Vanessa swabbed a boil on her neck, which had been lanced with a small cut to the infected area two days ago by Preston. 'Nice doctor, that Dr Lynley. Always has time to have a quick word. And so gentle. Ooh, it's a bit tender, dear.'

'Sorry, just a minute or two longer.' Vanessa listened, concentrating on the nasty infection which was in the process of healing but very slowly.

'Should be married of course by now—have someone to look after him. Still, I don't expect he's come across the right one yet. You married, are you, dear?'

Vanessa smiled as she applied the last of the antiseptic solution. 'No, I'm not.' And to make sure that the topic was not pursued she went on to explain to her patient that it might be an idea to use an antiseptic in her bath or washing water to eradicate any remaining bacteria.

As ploys went it was fairly successful, although Mrs Grainger managed to extract her age and a little personal history before Vanessa managed to see her off.

Then later in the afternoon she was left with a yawning gap.

'Mind if I come in?' Preston stood at the open door and she rose. She gave a little shrug, at which he strolled in and closed the door behind him.

'How is your father?' she asked politely.

'On the whole, he's recovering well. . .' he shrugged '. . .from a stroke. Sorry I didn't have to time to speak to you before I went. It was all rather rushed. You got my message about Katie?'

She nodded. 'Yes, it's good news, isn't it?' She couldn't resist bringing up Liam Kettering. 'I didn't realise you'd begun his treatment,' she said coolly.

'I wanted to have a look at him, so I thought I'd do the treatment myself first time around. And you were busy when he came in.'

'But you remembered to tell him to tell me where the cream was for his eyes?'

He looked at her curiously. 'Yes. Why?'

She paused. 'I would rather you told me and not hear it through my patient. I don't think referring treatment third-hand is a very good policy.'

He quirked a brow at her tone, but he sat down in the patient's chair and crossed his legs. 'Well, now, don't you?' He drummed his fingers heavily on the desk. 'As it happens, you weren't around for me to tell—I came to find you, but you'd left. Passing a message through Liam was a one-off and I certainly don't propose to use any patient as an intermediary. Now, if you've finished splitting hairs, Val said you had a half-hour free?'

Vanessa swallowed—hard. Was she being unreasonably

pedantic? She didn't think she was but, then, she was so confused about her feelings towards him that she might be going over the top. 'I'm not sure if I have,' she answered shortly, and bent her head to search the names on her list.

'I double-checked, so you needn't bother scrutinising that. Now, will you sit down and stop standing there like a sentry? No one is going to disturb us for a few minutes.'

She sat, reluctantly, avoiding his gaze.

'About this morning. . .'

'I'm sorry I barged in. It's a mistake that, having made twice, I shan't repeat again, I assure you.'

'Which is why you've hidden in here all day? Deliberately, to avoid me?'

'I've been busy, that's all.'

He gave a deep sigh. 'Oh, Vanessa, you don't understand—'

'I assure you I do,' she contradicted him icily.

'Hell's teeth, Vanessa, come off that pedestal of yours and try to behave like a human being for once!'

'Meaning?' she gasped acidly, jumping to her feet.

He placed two very large hands on her desk, got up and shook his head. 'I know what you were thinking and I dare say you had every right to think it when you walked in on us. But, then, may I just remind you that after what happened with Charlie and the way you deliberately misled me you really haven't got room to make judgements. So, if I were you I'd listen before wrinkling that pretty little nose of yours in disdain!'

It was the remark about deliberately misleading him which really provoked her and she glared angrily at him, her grey eyes glittering.

'Well, at least I have your attention,' he sighed and drove back the hair from his forehead with an angry hand. 'Now, for what it's worth, Caroline and I aren't involved—whatever it might have looked like. Caroline is a friend, as well as a colleague. She was—'

'Crying into your shoulder?' Vanessa offered crisply.

He nodded, straightening his back, and his green eyes narrowed as he stared at her across the desk. 'Yes, if you like. She's upset and, as it happens, her problems do involve me to some extent.'

I'll bet they do, Vanessa thought bitterly and stiffened her back, tilting up her chin as she met his gaze.

'But not in the way you think.'

'I'm not thinking of either you or Dr Grey,' Vanessa told him primly, folding her arms across her chest, 'but of my patients. May I remind you, Dr Lynley, that we both have surgeries for the rest of the afternoon?'

He shook his head again, sighing deeply. 'What is it that you have against me, Vanessa? Why don't you just come right out with it?'

'That's absurd,' she protested shakily. 'Utter rubbish!'

'Is it?' He stared at her, searching her face until he finally said in a low undertone, 'You might as well know that we may have the inconvenience of being one doctor short here soon. And it may very well affect your surgeries insofar as referring your patients to a female doctor.' At her astonished gaze, he gave a dismissive shrug. 'You obviously don't want to hear about it from me, so you'd better talk to Beth.'

And with that he left the room, closing the door behind him with a sharp thud.

CHAPTER SEVEN

A DAY later Vanessa found herself sitting in Beth's office, aware that she had been the world's worst fool.

Presumptuous fool too.

'Beth. . .' Vanessa hesitated '. . .can you possibly run that past me once more?'

Beth nodded, leaning forward with a frown. 'Just as long as you're aware that Preston asked me to keep this in confidence, Vanessa. It wasn't even brought up at the meeting.'

Vanessa flushed. 'Yes, of course. But I'm afraid I disturbed Dr Grey and Dr Lynley in. . .er, conference,' she said and, seeing the other woman's curious expression, added carefully, 'Dr Grey was very upset. I just happened to walk into his room at the wrong time.'

Beth sighed. 'Well, it could have happened to any one of us, I suppose. The tragedy is that Caroline and Mike are such good doctors, and this is a new practice with so much potential. Unfortunately, though, some difficult decisions must be taken soon. Mike and Caroline have to decide whether their relationship is over. . .' She shrugged. 'The likelihood is that one of them will leave. We desperately need a female doctor and yet Mike has a young family to consider. . . It really is such a pity.'

Vanessa sat there, utterly shocked. She had had no idea that Mike Shelley and Caroline Grey had been involved, and that Preston had been trying to talk some sense into her and Mike for the last year. Of course, now she could see it all clearly. But it had been so easy to jump to the wrong conclusion.

'So what are we going to do in the meantime?' Vanessa asked in dismay.

'I would advise you not to refer to Caroline anyone who would like a permanent female doctor,' Beth said cautiously, 'just for the moment.'

Vanessa nodded. 'I see. Well, it might be difficult, but. . .thanks, Beth.'

'Sad, isn't it? Two fine careers. . .two lovely people. The ways of the heart can be very cruel at times.'

'Very.' Vanessa got up to go, then hesitated. She looked back at Beth and frowned. 'Beth, were you working for the practice two years ago, by any chance?'

'I've been with Dr Lynley and Dr Grey since we opened, five—almost six years ago now. Why, Vanessa?'

Well, it was now or never, Vanessa thought, and since she was speaking in confidence to Beth she might as well ask. 'I was wondering if you might recall a member of my family who attended this practice two years ago.'

'I might,' Beth nodded, frowning thoughtfully.

Vanessa felt her pulse race. 'While I was in London my sister, Tara, wrote to me that she was undergoing private treatment with a doctor who specialised in sports medicine. Tara had a spinal problem, caused by a riding accident when she was young. She wanted to ride again, but it was always painful to sit in the saddle for very long. . .' She hesitated, beginning to feel embarrassed at Beth's curious stare. Then, quite suddenly, Beth's eyes widened.

'Did you say Tara? Would that be Tara Perry, the young woman who so tragically died after being thrown by a horse?'

'Yes. Tara was my twin.'

Beth's face sobered. 'Oh, Vanessa, I hadn't put two and two together. I'm sorry.' She gave a deep sigh as she sat back and drummed her fingers on the desk. 'I do remember the case, though I didn't know your sister personally. She was, in fact, Dr Grey's patient, I think. I can check on the computer for you, though of course all her records will have been returned to source.' Without waiting for Vanessa to reply, Beth turned to her computer, and after a few moments nodded. 'Yes, she was Caroline's patient.'

'You haven't a record of her seeing Dr Lynley on a private basis?'

Beth consulted the screen once more. She shook her head. 'No, there's nothing there. I don't think I remember Preston ever mentioning it. I'm pretty sure he only sees people he knows from the States who he feels committed to treat because of the personal contact.'

'I see.' Vanessa nodded thoughtfully. 'Thanks, Beth. You've been a great help. And er. . .all that we have talked about is in confidence?'

Beth nodded. 'Of course.'

At the end of the day Vanessa sat in her car and gazed across the deserted car park. Had she misjudged Preston so badly? Apparently Tara had not seen him on a private basis but in her letters she had been quite specific. Why, in that case, had she asked for money for treatment she had never undergone?

When she reached home the flat was deserted, and the first thing she did was to make herself a strong black coffee. Then she went to her room and dived into a shoe-box in the bottom of her wardrobe to unearth Tara's letters. Summoning her courage, she began from the very beginning to read them once again.

It was a week later when Tim's results came through. A knock came on her door, and when it opened she was surprised to see Preston standing there. Since the argument over Caroline she had seen very little of him and she studied his face anxiously.

'Tim's results,' he said and hesitated before coming in. 'I thought you might like to know what transpired.'

She nodded and stood up. 'Yes, I would.'

She knew very well that it was up to her to apologise over the wretched business of Caroline and yet she hadn't been able to bring herself to do it. He must know by now that Beth had enlightened her on the situation and she could hardly imagine that he would make it easy for her.

Still, perhaps this was an opportunity to try. 'Not bad news, I hope?' she asked, gesturing him to sit down.

'Not insofar as we can do something for him.' He sank heavily into the chair. 'The preliminary examination of the inside of Tim's knee, using the arthroscope, show that the cartilage or menisci are the root of the trouble. They've either been crushed or twisted and they've gradually begun to disintegrate. In fact, it appears that a fragment has been trapped in the joint.'

'Giving him such pain?'

He nodded. 'He must have been in agony, I should imagine, but still tried to play on—which didn't help matters very much.'

Vanessa sighed. 'He's so keen not to lose his place in the team, I suppose.'

'Well, that's beside the point now. Gavin Forth removed the menisci and the debris, but he's left the coverings of the cartilage at the ends of the leg bones within the knee. He's told Tim he's simply got to rest or he'll impair his performance—permanently!'

Vanessa nodded. 'At least the op will keep the joint working smoothly and relieve him of pain.'

'And provided he doesn't do anything rampantly unwise with the knee in the near future and gives himself time to heal he should be on his way to a full recovery. He'll have to be patient; miss a season. But he's young yet. And he's a bright future ahead of him if he's sensible.'

She gazed down at a pencil in her hand. 'Preston, while you're here, I think I owe you an apology.' There was silence for a moment and then she looked up and met his gaze.

'As a matter of fact, I have to disagree with you. You owe me two!'

'Two?'

'One for Charlie and one for Caroline.'

She crimsoned and nodded. 'You're right. I apologise for both misunderstandings. I shouldn't have jumped to conclusions over what I saw, and I should have explained about Charlie. What more can I say?'

'Be honest, Vanessa,' he continued in a low voice. 'You wanted me to think you were living with a man who was your lover. Obviously you wanted an excuse and Charlie happened to fit the bill. Why didn't you just tell me the truth?'

She chewed on her lip and shrugged. 'I suppose because I felt at the time it was the best way of discouraging you.'

He snorted. 'That doesn't quite tie up with your reaction when you supposedly discovered Caroline and I having an affair. Don't tell me you were affronted simply because of the embarrassment of walking in on us. Didn't your hostility towards me go a little deeper? Could it possibly be, as I suggested, and that you were jealous?'

'No!' she protested too quickly and then, realising her mistake, added evasively, 'I've apologised. Isn't that enough?'

He shook his head slowly. 'Not quite, no. I think you wanted a reason to keep me at arm's length because you found yourself attracted to me. And that scared the hell out of you. The question remains to be asked—why? Why are you so determined to keep me at a distance?'

He seemed to be able to look straight into her mind and home in on her most secret self, boring through all her emotional defences. Was he so determined to break them down because he felt that she had made a fool of him?

'I don't think we're helping ourselves by discussing

this,' she managed to mumble, taking a deep breath to calm herself and avoiding his gaze.

'Why not?' He quirked an eyebrow. 'Is it a bit too near the truth, Vanessa? Like nursing? For pity's sake, you're made to care for people, not to spend your life filling in forms and unravelling mountains of bureaucratic red tape. It's a gift you have and you're throwing it away.'

She stared at him, her throat tightening as her eyes began to fill. 'You haven't the right to say that. . .'

He frowned, his green eyes softening suddenly. 'I know enough about you to be absolutely sure there is only one profession in the world to fill that space inside you. And it isn't hospital management. Whatever it is you're running away from, Vanessa, you're heading in the wrong direction.'

For a moment she couldn't breathe, the air seemingly pushed from her lungs. Then, with an effort to stop herself falling completely apart, she shook her head firmly. 'I've made my decision, Preston, and I'm standing by it.'

He straightened, slowly sitting back in the chair to regard her as tiny white lines began to bracket the corners of his mouth. But the next shock was one she was totally unprepared for.

'In which case—now we know where we stand,' he enunciated carefully, his green eyes suddenly as sharp as emeralds, 'perhaps you would like to tell me the real reason you applied for this job? And would it have anything to do with the fact that Tara Perry was related to you?'

Vanessa sank back into her chair and told herself calmly not to be intimidated by the frustration and anger flooding into his face.

'Did you think I wouldn't guess?' he persisted, his voice gruff. 'Did you imagine I was that much of a fool?'

'I've never taken you for a fool,' she denied huskily, and when he didn't reply she lifted her chin. 'How long have you known?'

He got up and walked slowly to the window and gazed out, his back to her. 'Oh, I'm not sure, really. I suppose I began to suspect when you quizzed me on the issue of sports medicine. I put the name Perry to this and the way every so often you reminded me of someone I couldn't quite bring to mind.'

'And you didn't say anything?'

'Why should I? The onus is on you, Vanessa.'

She closed her fingers together in a firm clasp and tried to ignore the shake in them. 'I don't quite know where to begin.'

'At the beginning is as good as anywhere.'

She sighed and nodded slowly. 'Tara, as you may have guessed, was my sister—my twin sister—and she was a nurse too. Since Mum's death she'd been given to moods, sometimes deep depressions. Dad and I tried as best we could to coax her out of them, but it wasn't easy. And yet. . .she could be so bubbly and full of life—'

Just then there was a knock and Vanessa swallowed. 'Come in!'

Tina put her head around the door. 'Mr Crockett for a BP check, Vanessa. Shall I send him in?'

She nodded, rising wearily to her feet. 'Just give me a couple of moments, Tina, will you?'

Preston sighed. 'This is ridiculous, trying to talk here. We're going to have to sit down and resolve this without interruptions. I'm not on call on Saturday afternoon. I think we had better meet then,' he added gruffly, walking to the door.

She frowned. 'But, Preston—'

At that moment Mr Crockett appeared. 'Hello there,' he grinned. 'How are you two young people?'

'Fine, thanks, Mr Crockett.' Preston chatted briefly and then disappeared, leaving Vanessa to wonder what Saturday afternoon held in store for her. By the guarded expression in his eyes she felt the meeting did not bode well.

'How are the varicose veins?' she asked her patient as she took his blood pressure, forcing herself to concentrate on her work.

'Had it all done,' Mr Crockett told her happily. 'My specialist injected them with something to help them, apparently.' He lifted a leg, twitched up a trouser leg and displayed a neatly wrapped calf. 'I've forgotten the name of the stuff they put in the vein, but it's definitely helped.'

'I expect it's a sclerosant chemical which rectifies the inflammation and matting together of the vein walls. You've another visit to make, I should think?'

He nodded. 'Two more at Out-patients.'

Vanessa jotted down the satisfactory blood pressure reading. 'And what about your ulcer? Shall I have a look at it for you?'

Mr Crockett grinned. 'Oh, they did that in hospital too— said those dressings you've been putting on have done the trick.'

'That's nice to hear.' She helped him to his feet and walked with him to the door.

'Cheer up, Nurse Perry,' he grinned as she opened it for him. 'Worse things happen at sea, you know. Much worse.'

She laughed softly, managing to give him a bright smile, aware that her thoughts of Preston must have been engraved on her face and that she'd better do something about it—fast!

However, by Saturday the tension had merely increased as Preston had insisted on collecting her in his car from the flat. With her hair loose on her shoulders, she wore a soft blue cotton sundress and low-heeled pumps, though she had no idea where she was dressing for. Aware of his eyes going over her as she slipped into the car, she hoped that she had made the right choice. It was a lovely day, after all, and the sun kissed her bare shoulders as it flooded in through the windows.

She was alarmed, though, when he drove straight to Brideport General Hospital and parked in the car park. 'What are we doing here?' she asked in amazement as he turned off the engine.

'We've come to visit,' he told her mysteriously. 'Next, flowers.' He grabbed her hand and pulled her along and, dodging in between the cars, they finally reached the main entrance of the hospital, purchased a bouquet of summer flowers from the shop and then made their way out again to the pathway which, Vanessa remembered, led to the lake.

It was a fine day, if a little misty, a veil of vapour creeping over from the sea and hovering warmly in the tops of the trees—allowing a paler sun to break through in shimmering circles on the water. Around the lake there were many benches and on them sat patients, visitors and staff alike, leisurely enjoying the fresh air and the chance to breathe something other than hospital odours.

'Are you going to tell me where we're going, Preston?' She couldn't think why he had brought her here.

'To the eating disorders unit,' he told her. 'Duncrey Ward. Heard of it?'

Vanessa frowned. 'I don't recall it.'

'They floated it out as a six-monthly renewable experimental project. And I'm happy to say that, over two years later, it's proved so successful that they're keeping it. Here. . .' He passed her the bouquet. 'You'd better have these.'

Suddenly a young woman sitting on one of the benches waved to them, and Vanessa saw that it was Francesca Jay.

'Hello Dr Lynley. . . Nurse Perry.' She moved along the bench to allow them room to sit. Vanessa gave her the flowers.

'They're beautiful, thank you.' There was a little colour in the drawn cheeks and although she was still painfully thin at least a flicker of life wavered in her dark eyes. She was wearing jeans and a blue denim shirt and her brown hair was tied back in a ponytail.

'I've been looking forward to seeing you,' she said, and Vanessa realised that Preston must have forewarned her of their visit. 'It's nice to see people from the outside, and this is the first day I've been allowed out to the lake.'

Preston stretched a long arm on the bench. 'It's a bit gruelling, that first week of bed-rest, isn't it?'

Francesca shrugged. 'They told me it was necessary. I was upset at first. They put me in a room by myself. I didn't have a basin or a lavatory and I had to rely on calling the nurses. But they explained that it would be a temptation for me to vomit food or throw it away. Instead, they just talked to me when I began to panic.'

'And how are you feeling now?' Preston asked.

Francesca paused. 'I suppose I understand a lot more about myself. They try to give each of us individual attention and counselling. Everything is supervised—our rest, our feeding, our exercise. Sister will be here soon to collect me, but as I've been here three weeks I'm given a certain amount of trust.' Her voice tailed off to a whisper. 'But I don't know what will happen eventually. They tell us that true recovery only takes place when a mental readjustment happens. In my case,' she admitted candidly, 'I think I've a long way to go.'

Geese clambered from the lake and flapped around their feet. Vanessa realised that she still couldn't fathom why Preston had brought her here, but she was pleased he had. The girl seemed to be struggling hard to fight her disease and Vanessa was eager to give any encouragement she could.

'Here's Sister Miles,' Francesca told them as a small, neat-looking woman with short brown bobbed hair and dressed in a dark blue uniform came up to greet them. It was apparent that she knew Preston, but she smiled warmly at Vanessa.

'Tim is waiting for you in Duncrey, Vanessa,' she said. 'He's in a wheelchair and making a pest of himself,' she joked. 'Get him to help you find a vase for those lovely flowers.'

As Francesca turned Vanessa said, 'I'll come again—if you've no objection?'

Francesca smiled and shook her head. 'If you like.' As she walked away and pushed open the swing-doors which led to Duncrey Ward Vanessa's heart squeezed at the sight of the emaciated figure with the huge bunch of flowers.

'How is she doing?' Preston asked Sister Miles.

The older woman sighed. 'Early days yet. Even if she were to regain a normal weight and the doctor was reasonably happy that she'd achieved a psychological change, we are never surprised by a patient who recovers or relapses in a totally unexpected way. They sometimes discharge themselves without us knowing, even though we try to supervise them carefully.'

'And family?' Preston persisted. 'Any contact yet?'

'None,' sighed Sister Miles. 'The communication between Francesca and her parents broke down in her early teens and was never repaired. She gave us an address in Yorkshire but it turned out to be fictitious. As far as we can gather, the last medical records show an address in London.' She paused. 'Tim comes to see her each day, but he's only nineteen, isn't he? And he is being discharged soon. Who knows what might happen then?'

'I'm glad you brought me to see her,' Vanessa said when she and Preston were alone. 'But why be so mysterious about it?'

He leaned forward, elbows on dark cords, the soft, pale green linen shirt strained over his broad shoulders and his dark hair slipping smoothly over the top of the collar. 'Because if I told you you probably wouldn't have come.'

'Whatever do you mean? Of course I would have come to visit Francesca!'

He eased himself up and turned to look at her. 'It wasn't Francesca I was thinking of when I brought you here, at least, only indirectly. Vanessa, Tara was anorexic too.'

Vanessa stared at him. 'Tara, anorexic? You must be mistaken!'

He shook his head. 'I'm afraid not.'

'But I would have known—'

'Did you recognise Francesca as anorexic?'

Vanessa hesitated. 'No, not at first. . .'

'And how often had you seen her?'

She shrugged. 'Three times in all.'

'Exactly. And the last time was when she fainted and it was glaringly obvious to both of us that she was sick. Vanessa, anorexia is an illness managed on deception. The anorexic deceives herself and everyone around her. Even families fail to recognise the signs and very often don't know until it's too late. When your sister came to see me, before I transferred her to Caroline, she was dramatically underweight. Until Caroline managed to talk her into regular visits she was the same weight as Francesca. How long was it since you had seen her before her accident?'

Vanessa shook her head. 'A year, I suppose. I came twice in twelve months, but each time—'

'She had an excuse not to meet you?'

'Yes. . .yes. . .that's true. . .' Vanessa tried to grapple with the implication of what he was telling her.

'Which made you feel pretty bad when she had her accident? Feel guilty that you had neglected her in some way?' She nodded, the facts and fiction slowly falling into place. He reached out and took hold of her hand. 'You told me your father emigrated to Canada and that you had a sister. You explained that your mother had died when you were ten. When I weighed this up with the contradictory information Tara had given Caroline—that she was an only child of parents who lived in the West Country and were still alive—I realised that you probably had very little idea of Tara's psychological state at the time of her death.'

'But why—why would she lead a double life? Why would she lie to me?'

Preston shrugged. 'It might have been a way of recreating a past she felt she had been cheated out of. The anorexia was something she could control, something she felt a sense of personal power with.'

Vanessa stared blindly at the lake. 'But it's so hard to accept. I thought she burned off her weight—was one of those people who did.'

He nodded. 'With anorexia, the sufferer is profoundly influenced by the feelings and attitudes transferred from early important relationships, especially parents. None of us come out of a crisis unscathed. And, for Tara, anorexia might have been a way of coping with her loss.'

Charlie's words struck home then, for hadn't she said the selfsame thing when they had talked of anorexia? At the time her remark had not really registered. 'If only I hadn't gone to London. . .' Vanessa sighed and closed her eyes, putting her hands over her face.

'Tara was the only one who could have decided to change her life,' he told her gently. 'Not you or your father or a doctor. Francesca is here only because she came of her own free will. And, as Sister Miles says, who knows if she will stay?'

Vanessa flicked her damp eyes open and nodded, grateful for the comforting hand he had squeezed over hers. 'And here I was thinking I had such a lot to explain,' she sighed. 'And in an hour you've told me more about Tara than I ever knew.'

He smiled and pulled her to her feet. 'Come on, enough surprises for now. Let's find somewhere to eat.'

She stayed his hand, drawing him back to face her.

'Why,' she asked in whisper, looking up at him, 'are you going to all this trouble for me?'

'Why, indeed?' he growled, bending down to brush her lips with his mouth, and with a long finger slid the wisps of silky copper hair away from her eyes.

CHAPTER EIGHT

VANESSA lifted her chin, tilting back her head as Preston's lips moved softly over hers, her breath stopping briefly in her chest as the pressure of his kiss deepened and he drew her closer. She moved against him, sliding her hand along the hard ridge of shoulder, until suddenly a child's cry in the distance made them both aware of where they were and what they were doing.

He ran his hand along her arm. 'Let's find somewhere in the country. Make a change of scenery, shall we?' he said quietly and she nodded, sliding her hand into his as he led her back to the car, aware that neither of them wanted to speak but that the gesture of closeness as he walked beside her made her feel human again.

She was quiet as they drove, her mind replaying what she now knew, linking it with the many times she had been unable to grasp Tara's mood swings and her reticence to talk. Talk, as they had talked when they were children— before their mother's death.

They snacked on salads at a country pub and then drove into the downs where the blue sky met the rolling green hills with such clarity and freshness. Perhaps it was the after-effect of all she had learned that made her feel numb to its beauty, and she was grateful when he suggested that they walk for a while.

The footpath they chose after parking the car led them into woods at the bottom of a hill. He laid down a sweater in front of one of the huge trees and she sat, grateful he was not pressurising her to talk.

She leaned back against the warm wood and folded her arms around her knees, feeling as though she had so many questions she wanted to ask. 'I realise,' she said hesitantly as he sat beside her, leaning on one elbow, 'that Tara must have been sick for a long time.'

He nodded. 'I'm afraid so.'

She sighed. 'Tara wrote to me when I was taking my course in London. Dad and Jean had left for Canada and the house in Denton Road had been sold and she'd moved into a flat—she said. She mentioned a Dr Pres who was helping her with treatment. . .' she looked at him under her lids '. . .and that he was some kind of specialist in sports medicine.'

'Which is why you really came for the job?'

She shook her head emphatically. 'No. . .I had no idea Tara was registered with the surgery.'

'Until you recognised my name?'

She paused. 'Tara described a Dr Pres who was helping her to ride again and providing she had treatment—expensive private treatment—would be able to cure her spinal injury. She asked me for a cash loan for the treatment and I gave it to her. I thought it was really going to be able to help her. Until the next letter—when she asked me for a second loan.'

'Which you also gave her?'

She stared at him forlornly. 'What else could I do? She was my twin and I'd always thought it was my responsibility to look after her. She worked so hard—'

'Vanessa, Tara was unemployed. By her records, she hadn't worked in months when she came to us.'

'But she would never give up nursing. . .never!' She searched his face in disbelief.

'I would imagine she was trying to keep up appearances when she wrote to you.' He shook his head firmly. 'I didn't treat Tara privately—or in surgery—for a back complaint, and as far as I know she was not in employment when she made her visit and I saw her. She certainly wasn't nursing when Caroline took over her case.'

'You mean she deliberately fabricated her life—her whole existence—for my benefit?'

He looked away, narrowed his eyes and then, threading his hand through his dark hair, he turned back to face her. 'Vanessa, you must understand. Her motives were all part of the anorexia—the feeling of being in control and yet, paradoxically, a cry for attention. I think the money she borrowed from you simply went on day-to-day living. Tara came initially to visit the surgery with symptoms of depression, but I could see at once that they were linked to her physical state. I decided to refer her to Caroline because at the time Caroline was involved in the anorexia unit at Brideport General and would be the best person to help Tara.'

Vanessa hugged her knees once more, beginning to shiver. He drew her gently towards him and she leaned into him, her body moulding gratefully into his as he rubbed warmth back into her bare arm. 'But Caroline couldn't help, I suppose?' she murmured in a small whisper.

'I'm afraid not.' He squeezed her arm. 'Tara wouldn't accept that she had a problem. Caroline did all she could.'

Vanessa choked back a sob. 'Oh, Preston, poor Tara.' The sobs seemed to come unleashed from way down deep. He stroked her hair and kissed her wet cheeks and rocked her as the sun began to dip in the sky as they sat there in the calm, still wood.

It was late in the afternoon when she began to feel like walking again. When they finally reached the car she felt desperately tired and she must have shown it.

'Would you like to stop on the way back for a pick-me-up?' he asked her in concern.

She shook her head. 'No. I think I'd just like to go home.'

'Will Charlie be at the flat?' he asked as he slid in beside her.

'Probably. It's her Saturday off.'

He started up the engine. 'As long as you won't be alone.'

The drive home was beautiful with a summer sun filling the evening fields with a soft, golden warmth. But she felt so drained that she really couldn't enjoy it. Her mind wrestled with what she now knew about Tara and she had no doubt it was true. Perhaps, in her heart of hearts, she had sensed that something had been dreadfully wrong a long time before Tara's death.

Feeling deceived was the worst. That Tara had felt she could not share her troubles with the one person who loved and cared for her most. But, then, the anorexia had been so entrenched that it seemed probable that Tara, had she been well, would never have thought to deceive her as she had.

'I'll walk you in,' Preston said as they arrived in Chandler's Row. She let his sweater fall back on the seat and walked with him to the entrance of the maisonettes, feeling his arm wind around her waist.

At the door he laid a finger under her chin and tilted it up. 'I know this isn't the moment,' he said softly, 'but I think we need time to ourselves without ghosts.'

She looked up into the green, shadowed eyes. 'Preston—'

He laid a finger over her lips. 'Shh. Don't say anything tonight. In a few days life will seem a little brighter.'

He kissed her briefly and then turned, and she watched his tall figure disappear into the car and glide away into the evening mist creeping along Chandler's Row.

She hoped that Charlie would not be at home and she was truly relieved when she found a note saying that Ken had taken her to the cinema and she wouldn't be home until tomorrow.

Vanessa sank down onto the sofa and sighed.

At least she could lick her wounds in privacy.

The days passed and she found that Preston had been right.

Life did begin to look a little rosier. One Friday she had just finished her Well Woman clinic when the phone rang and she picked it up. 'Hi there,' Preston said. 'All done?'

'More or less. And you?'

'As free as a bird. Mike's on call for the weekend. As a matter of fact, I was thinking of eating out tonight.'

Her heart leapt. 'At Cosmo's?'

'How did you guess?'

'I could say telepathy.'

'You're making this incredibly difficult. . .'

'Am I?' she teased. 'Are you by any chance inviting me to dinner?'

'Would you accept if I were or would you be swimming or washing your hair or going out with Charlie?'

'None of those. And I'm ravenous.'

'Really?' His laughter came over the phone. 'Pick you up at eight.'

Three hours later Vanessa stood back from the mirror and debated whether she'd overdone the hair-do which she'd taken a patient half-hour to arrange on the top of her head in a coiled cinnamon knot which, despite its securing pins, still resisted its contrivance, and small copper tendrils escaped to fall stubbornly across her forehead and turn acrobatically over her ears.

Still, it had something. She'd leave it as it was. And the dress? Was it too formal for Cosmo's? The jade silk, figure-hugging and cut just above the knee and sculpted to her bare arms and neck, had been the dress she had bought at Christmas for the hospital party in London—to which she had never gone. Instead, she'd decided at the last moment to spend it with Charlie while Ken was on duty, and they'd celebrated Christmas in slippers and jeans with a giant bottle of Chardonnay in front of the tree in the flat.

Taking tiny jade drop earrings, she pinned them to her ears, completed the ensemble with slender heeled shoes and Charlie's black evening purse—which she'd left for her on the bed—and decided that there wasn't time to change even if she wanted to.

When he buzzed on the intercom she flew down the stairs, knowing as she opened the door that she had chosen wisely for he stood there in a delectable dark suit and crisp white shirt, daringly pinning a natty green spotted bow-tie to his collar. His eyes were almost luminous in their depths as he stared at her, and a whiff of something stunning made her take in her breath.

'Marks out of ten?' she asked nervously.

'Fifteen,' he answered and whistled a low compliment through his teeth. 'I don't think Cosmo's is quite ready for all this.' He gestured to her dress and lifted admiring brows. 'I think we might have to take a spin up to the Ritz instead.'

She laughed softly. 'Don't tease.'

'I'm not,' he said quite seriously. 'I mean it. I think we deserve a weekend away. . .catch a show. Wine, dine and dance until the small hours?'

Her face was startled. 'Preston, I don't think—'

'It's all right,' he laughed and took her elbow. 'Don't take me too literally.'

Was it a pang of disappointment she felt as he guided her towards the car? Couldn't be. And if he hadn't been teasing her she would have only refused anyway. It was just that for a few seconds there she had been tempted by the suggestion—a suggestion which was just enough to make her wonder what a weekend away with him would be like.

In the car she thought she had begun to relax—until he

reached across and squeezed her hand. 'Relax!' he told her and laughed. 'You can stop clutching your seat now. Your belt should be enough protection at forty miles an hour.'

She found herself laughing too and, remembering the last time at Cosmo's, felt a shiver of excitement run through her.

Cosmo welcomed them personally. He had prepared the same table for them—only this time with red napkins instead of white, red candles and two red roses in a slim vase in the middle of the table. As they sat down he lit the candles and explained that tonight he had a special treat for them.

Vanessa blushed as she watched him scuttle away. Only to blush even more deeply when he returned with an ice bucket and a bottle of champagne. 'For the beautiful couple,' he grinned, pouring them each a full glass. 'With the compliments of the house.'

Preston quirked an eyebrow. 'And what's the occasion, Cosmo?'

'Just that you have brought the *signorina* once more.' Cosmo grinned as he languished a twinkling gaze on Vanessa before flourishing his way back to the kitchen.

'I'll drink to that.' Preston raised his glass and stared over the rim at her, his eyes glinting as he surveyed her across the table. 'To us, Vanessa. At least, to this evening?'

It was tempting to raise her glass and meet his gaze and for a moment she hesitated, her fingers tightening around the stem. But she had the distinct feeling that if she did he would read more into the gesture than she meant. Instead, she smiled and remarked on Cosmo's thoughtfulness. Then she sipped and let the liquid trickle slowly down her throat.

She was thankful when Cosmo served first a succulent cantaloupe melon garnished with Parma ham, followed by

Zucchini alla Cosmo, a delicious courgette and Parmesan bake. Had she caught the flame of devilment still burning in Preston's eyes? she wondered. She decided that she had as every so often his eyes came up to hers, wildly exciting eyes which gleamed and flickered intimately in the candlelight.

'Worth coming?' he asked as they finished the last scrap.

'Absolutely. It was wonderful.' Vanessa sighed contentedly, unable to remember when she had eaten anything quite so delicious.

He crossed his arms on the table and studied her, his mouth turning up sensually as he licked his lips. 'In case you hadn't noticed,' he murmured softly, 'I've stayed out from under your feet for two whole weeks.'

She nodded with a wry smile. 'Yes, I'd noticed.'

'You needed a breathing space, I thought.'

She fiddled with her fork, not meeting his eyes again. 'Yes, I think I did.'

'Did? Past tense?' he inquired softly.

Colour flashed into her cheeks. She didn't know how to answer him and she was afraid to look at him to let him see what an effect he was having on her. Could he hear her heart pounding? Could he sense the cocktail of emotions he was precipitating inside her just by looking at her like that?

She felt him sit back, still staring at her. 'I think it will probably be Mike who leaves us, incidentally,' he said suddenly. 'Not Caroline.'

The moment he said her name Vanessa was aware of a sharp pang under her ribs, an ache which she had felt before and which she could not reasonably control. She couldn't help but wonder how deeply his feelings ran for the woman he had known all these years and with whom he'd created the partnership. Was it relief she heard in his tone that it was Mike going and not Caroline?

'Mike's a good doctor,' he went on. 'He's well liked and his patients will miss him, especially as a small ops man. But he won't have it that Caroline sacrifices the partnership.'

'When is he planning to leave?' she asked quietly.

'We've a new locum beginning in October. Once Mike finds himself another practice. . .' he tailed off.

'I'm sorry,' Vanessa said, genuinely upset for she had grown to like Mike a lot. 'Just when things were going so well.'

'We had such high hopes for the future. It's so damn disappointing. But I have to say that, if it came to the crunch, I would have hated to lose Caroline.'

Again the unwanted dart of jealousy stabbed at her ribs. 'Have you heard from your parents yet?' she asked, changing the subject quickly, unable to handle what she knew was an absurd and foolish reaction.

He nodded. 'My father seems to have made a good recovery, by all accounts. My brother and his family travelled over to see them and they spent two weeks sight-seeing.'

She looked up him. 'Not the ideal way to convalesce.'

He laughed softly. 'You can't go to Greece and not see something of the culture. It's the most beautiful place on earth. When we were training Caroline and I spent several summer breaks there, just island-hopping. It was incredible.'

Vanessa stared down at the white tablecloth in profound dismay. She found herself twirling the red napkin between her fingers until it was almost in shreds. 'I've never been to Greece,' she told him.

'Then perhaps you'd like to see it one day?'

She looked up and saw him watching her. 'I. . .I don't think I'll have time for a holiday this year. I'm due to start in London the second week in October. Things will be pretty busy. . .'

'Of course.' He nodded. 'I'd forgotten for the moment. It seems as though you've always been here. Time seems to have flown since that first day on The Point.'

Vanessa found herself agreeing. Time had flown. But at least in these few months she had brought to a conclusion the chapter in her life with which she had been so unreconciled concerning Tara.

Now she could look ahead—to her new career and to the challenge it offered which would take all her time and energy. And that was how she wanted it. For the first time in her life she was free and without family responsibilities. She wanted—needed—to devote herself to a fulfilling and exciting new role. And she knew that London offered her the very opportunity.

'I shall be sorry to leave,' she admitted, almost afraid to meet his eyes.

He dabbed at his mouth with a napkin, his eyebrows caught together in a frown. Just as he was about to say something the dessert arrived in the form of two Neapolitan ice-creams, and Cosmo surfaced once more to ask them if the meal was to their liking. When they had been left alone they began to eat and the atmosphere seemed to have changed.

'What are you thinking?' he asked her suddenly.

She smiled. 'I'm thinking what a lovely evening this has been.'

He grimaced. 'That sounds terribly final to me.'

'Preston, I don't want to mislead you—'

'About what?'

She shrugged, his question unsettling her, but he took her hand and held it.

'Listen, I'm not asking for more than you want to give this. . .friendship of ours. We can either carry on and enjoy our excursions out together or we can take the relationship further—for the rest of the time we've left to us. Either way, there is no gun at your head, Vanessa. I want you to be happy. The question is, what do you want?'

She knew what she wanted at this moment. She met his eyes across the table and her heart leapt. She might regret this for the rest of her life but she felt reckless and somehow bewitched, unshackled either by the past or the future.

'Will you see me tomorrow?' he asked her, his eyes roaming her face intently. And Vanessa said yes.

Not only did he see her on the following day, which was Saturday, but all of Sunday too. They swam in the sea, picnicked on the cliffs and drove again into the country. They met each other twice during the next week and again on the Friday for dinner at Cosmo's, this time a little less exotically dressed since they both went straight from work.

On Saturday morning Preston was on call, but he called at the flat for coffee to tell her that Katie had gone in for the biopsy. Together they went to see Sonia, who invited them into the garden to sit in deckchairs, and she explained that she was visiting the counsellor with whom Preston had put her in touch.

As they left Sonia's and climbed into the car he turned to her. 'What do you think?' he asked, leaning an arm on the wheel pensively.

'About Sonia? I think you were right. She did need help. At least she seems reconciled to the possibility of it being Still's now.'

He nodded, a slow grin coming over his face. 'How would you like to see a film this evening?'

She was almost growing used to his asking her out. It was the strangest of sensations and yet it felt so right. 'I'd love it,' she smiled. 'But aren't you on call?'

'I finish at six. Call for you at seven, OK?'

She agreed and he dropped at the flat, flying off to his next call. She spent all afternoon fussing about with her wardrobe and finally ended up choosing a long cool skirt in a summery cotton print and a silk blouse in a pale grey which set off her light tan. She let her hair loose to skim her shoulders.

'You look good enough to eat,' was his teasing remark as he collected her. 'I think I'll forgo the popcorn and the lollies and concentrate on you.'

She couldn't imagine him eating a lolly, or popcorn for that matter, certainly not in the trousers he wore in dark, immaculately creased linen and the soft shirt in a blue cord which contrasted intriguingly with his green eyes as he laughed and led her to the car.

They watched a box office hit, a gripping film of love and intrigue and obsession. When they walked out, Vanessa felt she had been on a long journey and was still up there in the clouds. He slid an arm around her waist and they walked down to the sea and strolled on the promenade beneath the cliffs.

The moon was full and a silvery blue and danced on the water as they stopped to stare over the ocean.

'What would you like to do?' he whispered in her ear.

She nestled into his warmth as the soft breeze kissed her skin. 'Oh, I can think of a million things on a night like this.'

He groaned. 'I don't suppose one of them would be eating a dish of tagliatelle and cracking open a bottle of Frascati at my place?'

There, it had come—as carelessly as the breeze which lifted the waves—a simple request which begged only one answer if she was wise. If she went back to his house. . . there would be only one outcome. She knew what she wanted to say, but it was the opposite to what she said.

'I'd like that,' she murmured and gazed up into his eyes and in the moon's light she could see her reflection. 'I'd like that very much indeed.'

He made them a supper of mixed salad, pasta and hot, crusty bread. They sat not in the dining-room but at the breakfast bar once more and drank a glass of cool wine with their meal.

Then they piled the dishes into the dishwasher and took coffee to the drawing-room. 'Music,' he said and went to a cabinet and began to fiddle with knobs. A love theme began to filter around the room.

The soft lighting enhanced the atmosphere and he came back to draw her down onto the huge chocolate settee and wrapped her into his arms as she lifted her feet and curled beside him. They sat in silence for a while and his long fingers played with her hair. She closed her eyes and listened to the music, aware of the thud of his heart next to her ear and aware, too, of her body's trembling response to his touch.

'What would you like to do tomorrow?' he asked as he teased her scalp with his fingertips.

'Are you free?'

'Mike's on call. We've a whole day ahead of us... unless you want to make it longer?' His hand slipped lightly to her neck and then cupped her shoulder and stayed there as though he was waiting for her reply.

'Preston...' she murmured and turned in his arms. 'If you mean—'

'I do mean,' he whispered huskily. 'But if you don't want what I want then I think, my darling, I had better take you home now. And we both know why.'

Her heart had begun pounding so loudly that she couldn't think. What did she want? Wasn't it perfectly plain to both of them what she wanted—why she had accepted the offer to come here? And yet even now he was giving her an opportunity to say no.

'Preston, I can't make any promises...'

'I'm not asking for any. I want you, my love. You know that, don't you?'

Oh, she knew it. Whatever was between them was too strong and too urgent to ignore or to deny. Whatever her

sensible, oft-repeated reasons were for not becoming
involved they no longer seemed to matter, not at this
moment. Not when she lay in his arms like this, aching
to be made love to.

'And I want you,' she whispered as he drew back her
hair from her face and bent his head to kiss her. The kiss
was slow and sweet, his tongue flicking out to challenge
the softness of her lips which parted hungrily, allowing
him blissful entry. The kiss was so welcome, so wanted,
so right for the moment that she slipped her fingers across
the arch of his strong neck and drew him down. The feel
of his body was as she had imagined it to be—lean and
heavy against her breasts, the firm planes of muscle tensed
and powerful against her legs

Vaguely she remembered thinking that the settee was
accommodating enough to make love on, and yet where
seemed unimportant now for they were locked together in
an embrace of deep and urgent need. But slowly he eased
himself apart from her. His eyes were dark and sensual in
the mellow light of the room, their hoods heavy with
arousal.

'Let's go to bed,' he whispered. 'I want to make to
make love to you, my darling, and I want it to be right.'

White satin? A woman's taste?

It was the first thought that went through her mind
as he laid her down on the bed. White satin sheets and
pillowcases. But she dismissed it quickly, knowing that all
she wanted was this—the moment she had been denying
herself for so long.

In several, swift movements he had thrust the door
closed behind them, laid her on the bed and moved to
switch on the subdued lighting. He stared longingly at her,
watching the fast rise of her breasts as she awaited him.

'I want you so much,' he groaned.

She opened her arms and he went into them, kissing

her urgently—his hand slipping down to her blouse and sliding it from her shoulders. His fingers seemed so practised and skilled and she blushed as he slid off her blouse.

'Preston, it's an eternity since. . .' she found herself apologising, aware that her cheeks were burning as he stared at her. But it wasn't her cheeks he was staring at. It was the full swell of her breasts which peeped out from the white lacy bra as he unclipped it. 'My darling, you're wonderful. . .perfect.'

Was she? she wondered doubtfully. So little a part of her life had been devoted to sex, to the enjoyment of the flesh and its pleasures. And it was never more evident than now when she gazed at his body and longed for him, suddenly anxious that she would not be able to satisfy him.

Her heart turned over as he dispensed with his clothes. He had a beautiful body, sleek and strong and, as he lay beside her naked, incredibly male. He was brown and hair-strewn and vibrant with life, as though the force of life itself rippled under the strong, honed muscle.

He removed her skirt with slow, languorous strokes as he rippled it down over her legs and over her small feet. Her slightly tanned skin glimmered in the soft light and he slid his hand along the nakedness of her thigh.

'I want you so much,' he said with raw emotion in his voice. The air trembled around them as, with a rasp in his throat and a low moan, he pulled her against him and they were joined—their bodies locked together, their mouths tangled in a kiss of passion and need. Her hips lifted against his and he smoothed her hair as he held her head between his hands and kissed her ever more deeply.

'Oh, my darling, I was so worried you wouldn't want this.'

Suddenly all her self-consciousness vanished as she knew how right this was. She met his eyes, those deep green, gemstone eyes so full of tenderness and passion. Their expression found an echo in her own heart. 'Oh, I want you, my darling,' she whispered achingly. 'I want you so much.'

His mouth found her breasts and explored them as she arched against him, their tiny buds standing to attention at the sudden attention lavished there. Then he slid lower, his mouth trailing soft kisses over her ribs and hips, melting her with fire as they found a lingering way across her abdomen in slow, delirious anticipation, teasing her thighs. . .and on to secrets she had never known existed.

When she could bear it no longer she cried out and he slid up beside her, whispering raggedly, 'Wait, my love, we must be careful.'

Soon he was beside her again, teasing the same sweet path along her neck and ears to her gasping mouth. 'Now, my sweet, now,' he groaned, but the pleasure was almost too great and she lost track of time and place, filled with joy and wonder. The ache of loneliness, which had been there before he had come into her life, was now banished as though it might never have been at all.

She lay in his arms and listened to the deep, constant breathing beside her.

Her cheek lay against the pillow's softness and in the darkness she felt him stir beside her. He slid his arm around her waist. 'You're awake?'

She smiled into the pillow. 'Yes, I'm awake.'

'Not lying there regretting?'

She gazed into his darkened face and wound her arms over him. 'No, not regretting,' she whispered. 'Not at all.'

She heard him sigh softly. His hands slipped down to the small, neat curve of her bottom and he drew her towards him. 'I want tonight to go on for ever,' he whispered tenderly and began to kiss her, nuzzling the smooth skin behind her ear and burying his face in her hair. Taking her cheeks between the palm of his hands, he kissed her again. 'I want to wake up in the morning and find you lying there beside me. I want to know what it's like to take you in my arms fresh from sleep. . .'

She trembled beneath the soft velvet smoothness of his tongue as his mouth marauded gently over her skin until she was mindless with ecstasy.

'Just feel what you do to me,' he whispered and moulded her to him, and she sighed with pleasure. Her fingers threaded through the soft, dark hair and she felt him shudder too.

And, with a ragged sigh, his tongue sought hers and the mad, aching fever began to grip her once more, until nothing mattered in the world except the moment and their need.

CHAPTER NINE

SUNDAY bells pealed across the town as Vanessa lay in the big double bed, wondering where she was. White satin stroked across her breasts. A long window with its vertical blind half-open and the breeze blowing through it. A strange and masculine bedroom and the space beside her empty. And then she saw Preston, fully dressed in tan Bermudas, T-shirt and thongs, leaning against a wall with his hands thrust in pockets as he studied her.

'Preston. . .?' She sat up in a panic and tugged the sheet across her breasts, her hair in a wild, coppery tangle around her head.

He was beside her in a second, his eyes warm and soft as he took her in his arms. 'Good morning, my sweet.'

She buried her head into his shoulder, beginning to take in her surroundings as memories of last night flooded back.

'I can hear that little brain of yours ticking.' He kissed her gently, turning her face up to him. 'I asked you last night if you had any regrets and you said no. Have you changed your mind this morning?'

She shook her head. 'No, no. I couldn't think where I was for a moment, that's all.'

'I was watching you. Drinking you in. Your hair over the pillow, your mouth so vulnerable in sleep—so beautiful. It took all my will-power not to come over and disturb you.'

'You should have. I. . . I've slept too long.' She blushed under his scrutiny. 'You're washed and dressed. I feel at a disadvantage.' She pulled the sheet up to her chin as she wriggled back into the pillows.

'It's the most advantageous disadvantage I've ever

seen,' he teased her, running his eyes over the slender and enticing form beneath the sheet.

'If I was more awake I could argue with that,' she murmured.

'You have the choice of arguing with me all day, if you like.'

She giggled. 'Can you be more specific?'

He nodded. 'Oh, yes, definitely.' He pulled her back into his arms and kissed her thoroughly. 'Is that specific enough for you?'

'Possibly,' she giggled, managing to get her breath back. 'Have you any more demonstrations in mind?'

'Well, you can have another if you like, right now, before we go out to eat breakfast.'

'Go out?' She wound her arms around his neck and sighed seductively.

'On the other hand. . .' He fell back with her onto the bed and began to unravel her. 'You're going to have to wait for breakfast.'

'You are my breakfast,' she told him and squealed at the hand which wriggled under the sheet.

It was the middle of the afternoon by the time they surfaced and the meal they ate was not breakfast, but a cream tea.

Vanessa had returned home to change into jeans while Preston waited for her in the car. As Charlie was still not back from Ken's she left a note to say where she was. She smiled a little at the mental picture of Charlie's face when she read the note and wished she could be there to see it.

The afternoon melted warmly into evening and Preston took her into the garden when they returned from their drive and they sat in the luxurious garden swing under a green and white striped gazebo. She talked of Tara again and of their childhood and she listened to what she imagined was an abbreviated account of Preston's austere upbringing.

The two boys had been sent to boarding school whilst their parents travelled in order to establish their property business. Preston seemed adjusted to this way of life, but she began to see that the independence he had earned at an early age was probably the reason he had remained a confirmed bachelor all these years.

They adjourned to the house and made love until the early hours. This time their love-making was slow and exploratory. She found herself hungry to experience his body, as he did hers, with a pleasure and satisfaction which made her forget everything else but the moment. At six-thirty in the morning he drove her back to the flat, kissing her lingeringly in the car before she unwrapped herself from his arms to hurry in and change for work.

Charlie was sound asleep. Vanessa smiled as she closed the bedroom door softly.

It was several days later before she bumped into Charlie again, this time at the supermarket. They collided by the frozen foods and both burst into laughter as their trolleys intercepted noisily.

'Of all the places to meet!' Charlie giggled. 'Where have you been hiding lately, you dark horse?'

'Where do you think?' Vanessa teased, lifting a brow.

'Really?' Charlie gaped at her. 'Well, about time too! Look, I've lots of news. When will you be home?'

'Tonight?' suggested Vanessa, recalling that Preston was on duty.

Charlie shook her head. 'No, I'm on lates.'

'Thursday?'

'I'm staying at Ken's. . .I'll ring you at work,' settled Charlie.

Vanessa was about to dash off but found herself reaching out to clutch her friend's arm. 'By the way, Charlie, did you know that Tara had given up nursing?'

Charlie sighed and lifted her eyes. 'I was wondering when you were going to ask me. I couldn't really help knowing, could I, since we both worked at the General? There were all sorts of rumours flying around. . .'

'About Tara?'

She nodded. 'I don't believe in spreading gossip, Van, but if you'd asked me I would have said. Who told you?'

She shrugged. 'Preston. Tara was a patient of Caroline Grey's, but she saw Preston once before he referred her. It seems you were right. He's never given Tara private treatment.'

Charlie sighed deeply. 'I'm sorry, Van. You're not cross with me?'

Vanessa smiled. 'For what? Trying to be tactful?'

Charlie rolled her eyes. 'That's a relief. Look, we'd better go or we'll be here all day chatting. Let's meet soon.'

Vanessa gave her friend a hug before they separated. Charlie had been a brick, especially since she and Tara had never got on. Tara's madcap behaviour had always been a bone of contention between them.

She was thinking about this later in the week when Preston came into the office. He wrapped an arm around her and kissed the back of her neck, then swivelled her into his arms.

'Is the door shut?' She tried to look over his shoulder.

'Wouldn't you like to know? Someone might come charging in just as I begin to kiss you. . .'

She remembered how she had felt when she'd walked in on him and Caroline. 'Preston, that's not funny.'

He chuckled. 'I'm quite beginning to enjoy making love to you in unusual places.'

'There's a name for that,' she reproved, melting at the sensations driving through her as he pinned her against the wall.

'It's called lust,' he murmured and kissed her again as

she blushed at the thought of an occasion only a few days previously. They had been walking through a wood and had sat down in a little copse where tiny silver birches had secluded them. Before she had known what was happening they'd been making love in broad daylight.

'You're laughing,' he complained, 'and I'm trying to make love to you.'

'Not here, you're not,' she giggled and pushed him away, just as Tina came bursting in.

'Dr Lynley. . .oh, I'm sorry!'

Preston brushed back his hair and Vanessa straightened her dress as discreetly as she could. 'Yes, Tina, what can I do for you?'

Vanessa decided that she would make an exit and left for her room. It couldn't have escaped Tina's notice that something was going on. Not that they had tried to hide what was happening—they couldn't. They spent every moment of free time they could together. Each time she looked at him and he smiled at her in that way she was sure the staff had noticed.

In her room she settled herself back at her desk and tried to attend to her paperwork but it wasn't long before Preston followed her, grinning all over his face. 'Now, where were we?' he threatened, striding towards her.

She lifted a book and waggled it at him. 'Stay where you are!' Then, more softly, she relented. 'What can your practice nurse do for you—in her professional capacity?'

He chuckled and leaned against the door, pushing his hands deeply into his pockets as he studied her. 'I've some news on Katie, actually. John Dale rang me and he's confirmed Still's.'

'Oh, dear,' Vanessa sighed, coming down to earth with a bump. 'Does Sonia know?'

He nodded. 'Sonia's taken it well enough, I suppose. They sent Katie to the dietitian straight away and she begins an initial course of iron injections, plus physio, which is all a bit daunting at first.' He paused. 'Come with me, if you like, when I visit.'

Vanessa nodded. 'Of course.' Just then her phone rang and as she picked it up and began to talk into it he came over and brushed a kiss on her forehead.

'See you later,' he mouthed and was gone.

She listened to Val explaining that she had a fifteen-minute break before the next patient and would she like coffee? But she couldn't concentrate on a word. When she put down the phone she sighed, thinking both of the Searles and of Preston. Deep inside her she worried. Whatever happened between her and Preston must come to an end.

And it was not as if he was pressing her for more. He seemed willing enough now to accept that she had a future in London and that she intended to stick to her plans. Not that the thought of hospital management seemed to give her much satisfaction when she compared it to the problem of the Searles, with whom she seemed to have become involved. But she had to remember what her aims were and how hard she had worked to achieve them.

She returned to her desk, picked up her pen and began to write, determined to keep her life in perspective and her heart under control.

It was on a hot, windless August day when they went together to see Katie and her mother.

'Looks like a storm,' Preston remarked as they knocked at the door. Just then a sheet of silver lightning stabbed through the dark clouds and thunder rumbled in the distance.

Inside the Searles' home Katie was playing with a friend. 'We haven't had any proper rain for weeks,' Sonia said abstractedly as they watched the rain begin to tumble from the sky, and the two girls pressed their noses against the window. 'Now it's the holidays it's probably going to pour.'

They sat down in the kitchen to the cold drinks she made. 'I'm getting quite proficient with the physio,' she told them. 'We do the joint exercises together, just as the physiotherapist taught us. But it's very tiring.'

'You're getting enough sleep?' Preston was watching her closely as he sipped his fruit juice.

'Well, I seem to lie awake and think about what might happen all the time. It's funny but before my therapy group I'd blanked off the worry and I slept quite well. But now everything seems worse at night.'

Preston nodded. 'Some people find they need less sleep or even resort to gentle exercise—something like yoga. What about going on a short course?'

Sonia turned her glass in her hands. 'Well, I'm thinking of a holiday, actually. My sister has asked us to go to Fretmouth to stay with them. It's only about an hour's drive along the coast, but it would make a change. We haven't been away for years, not since John took us to Devon when Katie was about two. I'm just worried that we'll be too much for my sister, what with Katie's diet and exercises. Or maybe she might have an attack there— her joints are really stiff at the moment.'

Katie and her little friend screamed at the window at a sudden clap of thunder and hurried back to the table.

'How are you, Katie?' Vanessa asked, noticing the child's sadly swollen knee and elbow joints.

'We might be going on holiday, mightn't we, Mummy?' Katie smiled.

'We might.' Sonia gave them a quick glance and Preston drew Katie onto his knee.

'May we have a quick listen?' He took out his stethoscope from his case and handed it to Katie. She showed it proudly to her little friend.

Vanessa realised again how wonderful he was with children. He handled Katie so gently as he perched her on his knee, and she responded quite happily as he listened to her chest through the V-neck of her sweatshirt.

Finally the children disappeared upstairs to play with their games in Katie's room. Preston wrote out a prescription for corticosteroids. 'If she becomes uncomfortable these will help to relieve the inflamed joints. She isn't complaining at the moment, but I shouldn't like you to be without something if you decide to go away.'

Sonia sighed. 'What do you think I should do, Dr Lynley?'

He paused as he packed away his case. 'I think you should go. Fretmouth's a lovely little spot. It'll do you both good. And certainly Katie likes the idea.'

She nodded. 'Well, nothing ventured, as they say.'

When they left and drove back to the surgery it was almost impossible to see through the deluge on the windscreen. The surgery was full of wet coats and umbrellas, and Val and Tina had switched on all the overhead lighting because it was so dark. A groan of thunder rumbled through the masonry and the lightning lit up the congested room with a sudden burst of brilliance. Preston gave her a crooked smile as they slipped off their macs and went to their rooms.

The rain continued unabated for the next few days, but it made little difference to Vanessa's frame of mind. The physical part of their relationship seemed to improve daily. They worked together well and, growing used to the new intimacy between them, they managed a fairly respectable façade at work. The only one she could not deceive was Charlie.

When she did return to the flat Charlie plied her with questions that she found hard to answer. Yes, she was still determined to follow her career. Yes, her plans were still set for October and nothing had changed.

'So you're content just to have a fling?' Charlie proposed one day. 'And plunge off in October, never to see each other again?'

Vanessa shrugged. 'You were the one who told me to enjoy myself!'

'But. . .that was before. . .'

'Before I actually took your advice?' Vanessa asked wryly.

'Well. . .' Charlie hesitated thoughtfully '. . .it's different now.'

Vanessa found herself dismissing the subject, but what Charlie had said played on her mind. Preston had given an added dimension to her life. But a relationship took honest commitment—she, of all people, knew that. Tara's short life and early death still caused conflicting emotions within her. How could she allow herself to be threatened again by losing someone she cared for?

It was during a cloudy Tuesday that Sonia phoned her at the surgery and explained that she had decided to go to Fretmouth for the last week of August. Vanessa told Preston as soon as he emerged from his room.

He nodded, smiling distantly. 'Good, they both need a holiday.'

She frowned. 'Is there something wrong?'

He raised a dark eyebrow and said quietly, 'I've just had Rachel Shelley in with me for the last half-hour.'

'Mike's wife?'

He nodded. 'Apparently, a local busybody saw Caroline and Mike together one evening. They told Rachel and she confronted Mike last night. Of course, he admitted the affair. Up till then she'd assumed that he wanted to move because he was unsettled at work.'

'Oh, Preston, how sad.'

'She says he's been desperately unhappy at home. Initially she put it down to stress. But last night he said he was unable to cope with the marriage any longer.'

'Even though he's leaving the practice?'

He sighed deeply. 'They've discussed separation.

Sixteen years of married life down the drain.'

'But surely there must be some hope for a reconcili-
ation?' Vanessa argued. 'After all, Mike was prepared to
leave the practice for his marriage's sake?'

'Rachel says he's devoted to the boys—they're fourteen
and fifteen. A difficult age, as it is. She feels they are the
reasons he's stayed and not her.' He shrugged helplessly.
'Rachel knew Mike was out on calls this morning and
came here to confront Caroline, but she collapsed in tears
at Reception and the girls wheeled her in to me. I'm just
going to run her home. Val's making her drink some tea
laced heavily with sugar.'

'And Caroline doesn't know she's here?'

He shook his head. 'No, Caroline's just left, thank God.
Which is probably a good thing for all concerned until the
situation has calmed down a bit. I can imagine Caroline
feels pretty devastated, too. I must try to see her.'

Vanessa made no attempt to say she felt that speaking
to Caroline would be unwise. Obviously he was close to
her. Much closer than she had ever imagined. Surely the
injured parties in this were Rachel and her boys? If anyone
needed support at this moment it was them.

'Well, I'd better let you go,' she said, trying to suffocate
the feeling she had that he wanted to hurry after Caroline.
The shuttered look in his eyes and the preoccupied
expression were things she recognised from Tara when
she wanted to hide her true feelings.

'Yes, I'd better go. Oh. . .' He hesitated, grasping her
arm. 'Can you ring Sonia for me and ask her to leave her
sister's number with us?'

Vanessa nodded, feeling his hand slip away and a coolness wash over her. She tried to put her concern from her
mind as she went and rang Sonia. After jotting down the
number she gave it to the girls in Reception, now empty
of visitors, aware that they were talking softly in whispers.

Was it pure accident that she overheard Tina suggest

that she had thought Preston and Caroline were made for one another? As she walked back to her room old doubts resurfaced from the first time she had seen Caroline in his arms. He could not bear to think of Caroline in distress!

It was as though the shadow of her fears now moved clearly into the focus of her relationship with Preston. She did not suspect him of unfaithfulness to her. Worse, she suspected that he did not know the depth of his own feelings towards the friend he had known for so long.

That evening she drove to his house. He was already there ahead of her, in boots and an open-necked shirt, clearing damp leaves into a heap at the bottom of the garden. He worked aggressively, his muscular arms tensing below the rolled-up sleeves of his shirt as he thrust a fork into the garden debris.

When he saw her he drew her into his arms and brought down his mouth in a hard and passionate kiss, holding her head between his hands so that her hair fell from its band and cascaded into a burning halo around her head as he ran his fingers through it.

'How are you?' she murmured, staring into the hollows of his face, where dark rings had begun to form around his eyes.

He shrugged. 'Trying to work off some excess energy, I think.'

'Because of what happened today?'

'Perhaps.'

She bit down on her lip. 'How is Rachel?'

He drew her to his chest. 'Miserable and lonely. I found a neighbour to sit with her until Mike arrived. Then I called back to see Caroline. She's distraught, of course. We talked. . .but she's too confused and upset to come up with any sensible suggestions.'

A cold shiver of apprehension ran down Vanessa's spine as a faraway look came into his eyes. She realised that

she had been right. Intuitively she had gauged the deep
feeling he must have towards Caroline.

'C-Caroline means a great deal to you, doesn't she?'
she said before she could stop herself and he held her
away from him at arm's length, a frown spreading across
his face.

'I care for her—about her, yes,' he admitted with a
puzzled frown. 'But, damn it, woman, what does Caroline
have to do with you and me?'

She didn't quite know how to reply to that, but fortunately she was spared a reply as, from inside the house,
the phone began to ring.

He let her go reluctantly. 'Come into the house,' he
said softly.

She knew what would happen if she did. 'You'd better
get the phone,' she said. 'I'll wait.'

'You had better,' he threatened gently and strode down
the garden, kicking off his boots at the French windows
and leaving her alone with her thoughts.

She stared at the broad back and the bowed shoulders
as he disappeared into the house. Her heart felt as if it
was twisting.

She stood still in the evening glow, listening to the birds'
song—bewildered by her scattered senses and confused
feelings. If she left now she might stand a chance of
assembling her thoughts into some form of coherence.

But she hesitated too long for he was soon hurrying
from the house in stockinged feet, striding across the lawn
to where she stood. Wrapping her in his arms, he heaved
a deep sigh. 'It's so good to have you here,' he whispered.
'I thought for a moment you might want to leave.' His
hands went softly over her hair. 'That was Caroline to say
she's going to take over the on-call. I told her I'd take it
if she didn't feel up to it. But she seems to want to try to
keep things as normal as possible.' He stroked back the
tendrils from her face. 'Which means you and I. . .' He

brought down his mouth searchingly over her lips and she tried to respond, whilst erasing the echo of Caroline's name from her mind.

Inside the house, the outside world faded as if by magic. She had long since ceased to tease him about the white satin sheets, of which the companion pair—in a deep red—were now spread across the double bed.

'Just for you,' he had told her with a rueful smile.

Oh, sweet words, she thought as he held her to him. But a man like Preston couldn't sail through life without emotional entanglements of some kind. Why not Caroline Grey? She was young and beautiful. And the affair with Mike might just be the storm in a teacup that Preston had once remarked he hoped it would be.

A thought which clarified into clearer perspective when she kicked off her sensible nursing shoes and trod across the thick pile of the carpet towards the shower, a thought which took the nubile form of Caroline Grey in this very room, her dark hair spread over the deep red pillowcase. Ridiculous, she hastened to rebuke herself. Even if Preston had been involved with Caroline during their training days, he was not now.

Or was he? Did she really understand how he felt? Two people who had known one another closely; two people on the same wavelength, companions from the past and partners of today. Perhaps neither Caroline nor Preston had been able to accept the depth of feeling which had grown during their long friendship?

And that was the moment when she realised why she had been so staunchly clinging to her plans for the future and avoiding falling in love. The giving of self in a relationship had only ever led her to pain. Vanessa swallowed, fending off the painful memories that surged through her as she recalled her mother's and sister's deaths. Even Dad had left Brideport and all its memories behind him to escape to a new life.

'Hey!' Preston caught her arm and twirled her around. 'Where do you think you're off to?' She jumped as he pulled her into his arms and she knew that, above all, she mustn't let him read her thoughts.

'I'm going to pamper myself,' she excused brightly, 'and use some of your extravagantly expensive shower gel.'

'And leave me like this?' He leaned her against the wall so that she linked her arms around his neck, knowing that she could never refuse him her body.

'I won't,' she teased softly, 'be very long.'

'Even five minutes is too long. Come to bed,' he whispered and she gave in. Her body ached for him, refusing to be quelled as had her mind and heart when she had refused to admit to falling in love—suffocating the jealous pang which had threatened to engulf her earlier.

He picked her up in his arms, lifting her easily to the bed. Slowly he began to undress her, his fingers moving over her blue uniform with a practised familiarity—sliding her belt from her waist, drawing the soft cotton over her shoulders. She barely remembered him undressing as her heart missed a beat at the strength and beauty of his presence as he lay beside her.

Her body thrilled instantly to his touch. He knew how to make her cry with joy and arch in delight to the stirrings of his own body. Or to hurry with the force of a gale into a headlong storm of passion which consumed them with a breathless and mysterious harmony.

He was the creator of the music of her soul and played her with such infinitesimal perfection that she was hungry each time for yet one more performance of their symphony together. Mornings always came too swiftly. Light always crept into their darkened nest too soon. And in the early, silent hours, even before the dawn chorus, Vanessa awoke to wish that she could remain, burning in the feverish flame of their desires yet another day and another night and another. . .

But now she knew for certain that it could never be. The pleasures he gave her would be memories one day. And they would be wonderful memories. She must be content with that.

CHAPTER TEN

IT WAS hard to believe that Francesca Jay had been in Duncrey Ward for eight weeks. Vanessa thought she looked better but still very thin, and Sister Miles had expressed concern that her weight was fluctuating. This was causing the team problems insofar as Francesca's confidence was not helped by the erratic visits of Tim.

Once more Francesca sat by the lake, and when Vanessa arrived she gave her a tearful embrace. Very soon Vanessa discovered that Francesca was about to discharge herself.

'I don't feel in control here,' Francesca tried to explain. 'At least when I eat what I want to eat I have this feeling that, whatever happens, *I* make it happen and not other people.'

'But, if you leave, where will you go?' Vanessa asked her.

'To Tim's. He says he thinks I'll be all right now.'

'But Tim has his own health problems,' Vanessa tried to reason, 'and there's the prospect of him not playing until next year. Have you thought he might not be able to cope with more pressures? In fact, he may well be expecting you to be able to support him. Do you think you're ready for that, Francesca?'

'But he's not keen on coming to the hospital. I'll lose him if I stay in here any longer.' Her voice was barely audible.

'If Tim cares,' Vanessa said gently, 'he'll wait for you. You have people here who understand anorexia and are trying to help you into recovery—a permanent recovery.'

'But what if he finds another girlfriend?' Francesca's thin lips wavered.

'Well, what if he does? Is it really the end of the world? You have so much ahead of you. Perhaps you can't see it at the moment but there is a future out there, possibly not with Tim but with someone who will love you and understand what happens with anorexia.'

Francesca kept her eyes on her lap and Vanessa sighed. She just didn't seem to be able to reach her. It was as if she was cocooning herself away from all help.

'My sister, Tara, had anorexia,' Vanessa said and realised that she had briefly gained the girl's attention when she looked up.

'Did she get better?'

'She had an accident, a fatal accident, two years ago. If she had lived I like to think she would have beaten the disease.'

'Which is why you're helping me?'

Vanessa smiled as she shook her head. 'I think it's the other way around. You've taught me a lot about anorexia—things I wished I'd understood for Tara'a sake. Have a little more patience. I'm sure all your efforts will pay off.'

Francesca's attention wavered. Vanessa turned to see what had distracted her. Sister Miles approached with a tall, gangling young man, his emaciated frame and dark-ringed eyes over hollow cheek-bones betraying the fact that he, too, was anorexic.

Sister Miles introduced Gary Evans and drew Vanessa aside, leaving Gary to sit on the bench beside Francesca.

'Gary's been admitted today, but he's been to Duncrey once before—in January. It didn't last long, I'm afraid—about a month. His wife left him while he was here.'

'Oh, dear,' Vanessa sighed. 'Virtually the same problem as Francesca. Did you know she wants to leave?'

Sister Miles nodded. 'She had a visit from the boyfriend last night and it ended in a terrible upset. Francesca was in tears. We've been trying to reason with her, but she's adamant she's going.'

Vanessa sighed and glanced back at Gary Evans, sitting on the bench. 'It's not often you find a man with such severe anorexia, is it?'

Sister Miles shook her head. 'No, we've not had many. But it is on the increase.' Then her brows lifted a fraction. 'I thought perhaps they might be able to find some common ground.'

'Hmm, maybe,' agreed Vanessa thoughtfully.

'Who knows?' Sister Miles chuckled wryly. 'Anyway, we don't ever give up here. We just take one day at a time.' She left then and threaded her way back through the visitors to Duncrey. Vanessa walked back to Francesca and Gary and said her goodbyes, mentioning that she would call again the following week—even though Francesca gave her a frown.

She finally drove back to the surgery through a sprinkling of rain. The downpours of the early part of August had finally abated. And as she drove into the car park a brilliant sun did eventually shine from behind the clouds.

Perhaps Sonia and Katie would have left by now, she thought as she put Francesca's problems on mental hold and walked into the surgery to find summer madness in process.

Caroline, Mike and Preston were flat out with lists stretching to the end of the day, and her own list was not much better. Her first patient was a holiday-maker, a man with a chesty cough which had developed into a chest infection, and Vanessa asked him to wait so that she could ask a doctor to see him.

'Not likely,' objected the man, and promptly explained that he was enjoying the local brew too much to mix with antibiotics. 'All I want is a cough medicine a bit stronger than you can buy in the shops. Can't you nurses give it?'

She smiled ruefully. 'I'm afraid I can't. But one thing

I can do is to assure you that your chest infection won't be helped by overdosing on beer.' He began to cough until he was almost blue in the face as he tried to leave her room. Vanessa imagined that he would have sneaked out from surgery but just then she heard Preston in the hall, and opened her door to find him talking with a patient. He turned and frowned at the coughing, lifting his eyebrows at Vanessa.

'I should get that seen to if I were you,' came the surprising observation of the small, rosy-cheeked woman Preston was addressing. 'Never put right tomorrow what you could today, and that's a fact I can guarantee from personal experience.'

Vanessa stared in surprise at Pat Sanderson.

'I've a couple of minutes' gap,' Preston intervened kindly. 'Would you like me to listen to that chest of yours?'

The man, faced with their united concern, nodded, albeit hesitantly, and Preston took the temporary resident slip from Vanessa. 'I think Mrs Sanderson here would like to see you.' He gave her a rueful smile.

Vanessa watched him guide the coughing man away and Pat Sanderson, bidding her good morning, walked cheerfully in and sat down, removing her cardigan.

Vanessa closed her door as the next to come off was a blouse, then a vest and finally a bra. Pat Sanderson smiled broadly at Vanessa, gesturing to a small set of sutures beneath her left breast.

'You've had the ganglion removed!' Vanessa stared in surprise.

'Well, I wouldn't have if it wasn't for you.' Pat Sanderson proudly showed off her scar. 'I thought about what you said and made an appointment with Dr Shelley. He nipped it off eight days ago. I've just had the laboratory results and it was all clear. Dr Lynley said you'd take out the stitches. I'm so relieved I can't thank you enough.'

'But I didn't do anything.' Vanessa led the way into the treatment room.

'You were nice, that's what,' Pat said as Vanessa slipped on sterile gloves and snipped away, releasing all four sutures cleanly. 'I plucked up courage and he took it off without any trouble. But after all those years of being terrified of doctors and nurses you were the one who really restored my confidence.'

Vanessa smiled. 'Oh, you'd have come along eventually. But I'm pleased you aren't terrified of us any more.'

'Anyway,' said Pat Sanderson as she dressed again, 'whether you like to take the credit or not, I've told Dr Lynley what I think. I think you nurses deserve a medal.'

Vanessa laughed softly, but inside she had a lovely feeling of warmth. It was the most wonderful feeling on earth, helping someone and, yes, being told so! A sentiment Preston echoed at half past five when he rang her on the internal phone and relayed his conversation with Pat. 'Apparently you've become indispensable to us, Nurse Perry,' he said. 'Therefore, as a small incentive to a valued member of staff, I thought about a bonus.'

'Bonus?' Vanessa grinned into the phone. 'What kind of bonus are you thinking of, Dr Lynley?'

'Do you remember we once talked about a weekend away?'

'The Ritz, wasn't it? And I was mad enough to refuse!' She sighed, stretching her weary back.

'Well, here's a second opportunity. How do you fancy a break over Saturday and Sunday? The West Country, perhaps?'

'You're serious?' she laughed.

'Absolutely. After all, we've only just over a month left. . .'

It hit her then, like an express train. A month to go. The smile slipped slowly from her face as she gripped the phone.

Suddenly the prospect frightened the life out of her. But it was what she wanted, wasn't it? She closed her eyes and snapped them open again as if to clear her brain.

'Anywhere special you'd like to go?'

'N-no,' she stammered unsurely. 'The West Country sounds fine.'

He chuckled. 'I'll see what I can do.'

When she replaced the phone she stared ahead blindly. It was almost over—her job here at the practice, Brideport, Preston Lynley. And the very worst thing was his apparent acceptance of it, she realised.

He had not brought up the subject of her leaving until today and that was only in a passing fashion. But, then, hadn't she been so absolutely convinced of her future, so determinedly geared to leaving this town behind her, that she'd not been at pains to disguise it?

He was obviously resigned to her going. Which, on the whole, should make leaving pain-free when it came. A thought which was not at all reinforced when she gathered her coat and bag and stared out of the window—just in time to catch Caroline Grey climbing into the Porsche beside him.

He rang her on Friday evening at the flat and made last-minute arrangements to pick her up at eleven in the morning. 'Packed your bikini?' he teased.

'Bikini, shorts, T-shirts—everything but the kitchen sink.'

'But not sweaters and macs?'

'Do you think we'll need them? The forecast is good. No more rain.' She was suddenly hesitant.

'We can always cuddle up to keep warm.'

'In that case, I won't bother with coats.' She frowned. 'You haven't said where we're going to exactly.'

'Curious creature, aren't you? Well, if you must know, I've booked us in at a romantic little hotel perched above the river Dart. Not so little, actually, as the bed is a four-poster. And, what's more, we're Mr and Mrs Smith.'

She burst out laughing. 'Oh, you idiot! I'll never keep a straight face.'

'You'll have to. This place is very selective.'

She gasped. 'But I've only packed jeans!'

'Then you'd better throw in something sexy and a pair of high heels. We're going to dine lavishly, then smooch the night away.'

'You could have warned me. I thought we were just going to be drifters on a beach all weekend.'

He laughed softly. 'The idea had a certain appeal, but the bed won in the end. Now, hadn't you better get some beauty sleep before tomorrow?'

'I shan't have time. I have to repack.'

He laughed and murmured huskily, 'Don't forget the black negligée.'

They ended up whispering crazy-sounding goodnights and Vanessa put the phone down just as Charlie came into the bedroom in her slippers and dressing-gown, pushing a cup of hot chocolate onto the bedside table.

'Don't forget your toothbrush,' Charlie giggled and sank down on the bed to watch Vanessa unlock her suitcase once more and push everything down to make way for several more dresses and a slinky black evening gown.

Charlie sighed. 'You'd better make the most of this, my girl, because your time's up soon. According to the gospel of Nurse Vanessa Perry, it's *adios, amigo* in just over a month's time.'

'I'm perfectly aware of how long it is, thank you!' She was aware that Charlie had been dropping hints about October like lead weights for the last week! 'And I intend to make the most of every moment. Remember, you were the one who advised me to have some fun.'

'I hope,' sighed Charlie and fixed her with a laser stare, 'that you know what you're doing.'

'I'm only going away for a weekend.'

'Not that. I meant London.' Charlie rolled back on the bed and gazed thoughtfully at the ceiling. 'My grandmother used to say, "Charlotte, be careful what you wish for, because one day you might get it."'

'And?' Vanessa stood with her hands on her hips.

Charlie sighed and pleated her fingers across her chest. 'Oh, nothing much, really.' She turned to look wisely at her friend. 'It's just that London might turn out to be an awfully expensive wish.'

The morning was filled with a bright sunshine which burst into the flat and sent sunbeams spinning all over the room. Charlie had thrown the windows open and the sound of the Porsche turning into Chandler's Row could be heard quite clearly as the machine purred to a halt beneath.

'Limousine's arrived!' Charlie leaned out of the window to wave to Preston.

Vanessa lugged her suitcase into the lounge. 'I think I have everything. Wait! Sunscreen!'

'You'll be able to buy plenty there.' Charlie lifted her eyes to the ceiling. 'Vanessa, you're going to be worn out by the time you arrive. You've been up since dawn wearing yourself into a frazzle.'

Vanessa took a last look in the mirror. 'How do I look? Do you think these shorts will crease?'

'You look perfect.' Charlie gazed admiringly, if ruefully, at the tall, slim young woman with abundant copper-coloured hair and huge grey eyes glimmering worriedly underneath its tangled effervescence. The beige shorts and soft green cotton top were the third change of the morning so far. She nodded enthusiastically.

Vanessa glanced at the overnight case. 'I've forgotten shoes!'

'No, you haven't. They're there. See? Sticking out of the side pocket. Two black heels and the top of an espadrille.'

'Heavens, yes.' Vanessa closed her eyes and sighed. 'I don't know why I'm so nervous!'

'I do,' teased Charlie and opened the door to Preston.

'Morning, Charlie.' He sauntered in and grinned rakishly. Vanessa thought he looked gorgeous. Buff short-sleeved open-necked shirt, casual fawn trousers and a drift of aftershave which curled around Charlie's nose as she wrinkled it.

'You'd better take her away,' Charlie suggested, 'before she wears herself out. I dread to think what she'll be like in October—' She grimaced, realising what she had said.

Vanessa cast her a killing glance and hauled her bag to the door.

'I'll take it.' Preston took it from her, apparently unaffected by Charlie's remark. 'My goodness, what have you got in it—the kitchen sink?'

'Almost,' offered Charlie with a giggle. 'But she couldn't get the zip over the taps.'

Preston laughed and made his way down the stairs.

'Sorry!' mouthed Charlie behind his back.

Vanessa realised that she was disappointed because Preston hadn't reacted. But what did she want him to do?

'See you Monday,' she said outside and gave her friend a forgiving smile.

Preston propelled her into the car. Soon Charlie was just a small figure waving goodbye on the pavement of Chandler's Row.

Preston flipped a map into Vanessa's lap. 'You're navigator.' He had seemed to have forgotten what Charlie had said. 'Any wrong turns and there'll be a forfeit.'

'Promise?' she giggled.

'You fancy a dunking in freezing cold sea?'

'It's not supposed to be freezing in summer.'

He laughed and stretched out a hand to cup hers. Then he frowned as a strange noise erupted from the back. 'Lord, what's that?'

She stared around. It seemed to be coming from the floor behind them.

'The mobile,' he grumbled and pulled in to the side of the road. 'I should have turned it off.'

'Are you going to answer it?'

He switched off the engine. For a moment he hesitated, then he pushed open his door, reached back in and jerked out a bag. Underneath it lay the phone. He looked up at her. 'I'll have to switch it off or answer it.'

Their eyes met over the bag.

'Is it the surgery, do you think?'

He grunted under his breath and she took it as a yes.

Slowly she reached around her seat, found it on the floor and handed it over. 'No peace for the wicked?'

He took it and listened, then stretched across to the pad and pencil he kept in the front. With one hand resting on the driver's seat, he scribbled down an address.

When he'd finished he looked up at her. 'Do you want the good news or the bad?'

'Is there any good news?' she asked suspiciously.

He sat back in beside her with a sigh. 'That was the coastguard's office. They believe Sonia and Katie are trapped in a cave called Froggat's Hole at Fretmouth. Apparently the tide came in and cut them off and a young-ster gave out the alarm. I know very little else, except that Sonia's sister phoned me because she had our number in case of an emergency.'

'How on earth did they get trapped?' Vanessa gasped.

He shrugged. 'They didn't know any more, other than the emergency services are all there. They're pulling out every stop to rescue them.'

Vanessa sighed as she looked through the windscreen into a perfect summer's day. 'Fretmouth's not far, is it?'

'About half an hour from here. I know Froggat's Hole. The tides are notorious there and if they've had a flash flood through the rain. . .' He left his sentence unfinished.

She reached out and closed her fingers over the firm muscles of his arm. 'Let's hurry, then.'

He leaned across and kissed her briefly, and the touch of his lips made a small shudder go through her body. She was beginning to wonder if fate wasn't telling her something. . .

Froggat's Hole was hidden under a small peninsula of land which rose from a sweep of marshland to a craggy head, sheltering rocky caves beneath. Vanessa had visited there once when she was a child on a school outing and now, as Preston drove the Porsche into the car park, she recognised the little café which served the tourist trade and was now, in the middle of August, bustling with activity.

The incongruous sight of a handful of police cars parked by the barrier which prevented traffic from entering the tiny lane winding up to the beach made her shudder.

'No traffic along this road today,' a police constable told them as they neared the group of vehicles.

'I'm Dr Lynley,' Preston told him as he lowered the window. 'I believe two of my patients have been trapped in the caves.'

The policeman flicked on his portable radio and spoke into it, then he nodded and lifted the metal barrier. 'One of the Land Rovers will take you down, Dr Lynley.'

No sooner than they were through the road block than another man came up to them and introduced himself as part of the emergency service rescue team. He showed them to one of the Land Rovers and they clambered in, and very soon were being driven along the narrow lane.

'What time were you alerted?' Preston asked.

'Ten, this morning,' the driver answered.

'And Mrs Searle and her daughter. . .?'

'As far as we know they're with two other people, trapped on a ledge in one of the caves. It's a popular beauty spot and easily accessible from the beach, but when the tide comes in it sweeps into Froggat's Hole and cuts the place off.'

'Who raised the alarm?' Vanessa leant forward from the back seat.

'A youngster, about sixteen. He swam under the pool in the cavern and surfaced the other side. He almost didn't make it.'

There was silence then and the Land Rover rumbled down the deserted path and finally came to a halt by a group of beach huts. The police had already cordoned off the beach with fluttering orange tape, and the only sightseers were those who huddled in a group a hundred feet above on the brow of the cliff.

The rescue team was gathered on the sand and the blue water was swirling around the small boats beached by the rocks, ready to take their passengers out to Froggat's Hole by motor launch.

'Dr Lynley?' a woman asked. 'I'm Gail Farnsworth and this is my husband, Derek,' she explained as a man approached. 'I'm sorry to drag you here, but I didn't know what else to do and the police said in view of Katie's condition it would be best to have someone. . .' She shrugged, holding back the tears.

'What exactly happened?' asked Preston.

Derek Farnsworth explained that they had come by car for a day's trip to the beach. They had set out very early to avoid the traffic. When they'd arrived they'd left the car in the car park and travelled by the little train to the beach because Katie couldn't manage a strenuous walk.

'It's my fault,' whispered Gail. 'I left Sonia and Katie playing on the water's edge. We'd forgotten cold drinks and so Derek and I went back up to the café to buy some for the day. I didn't think to mention to Sonia not to go around to the caves—I didn't think Katie would want to walk. . .'

Derek Farnsworth nodded. 'Sonia left the bags with a

lady who was sitting beside her on the beach. She said
Katie wanted to try to walk along the beach. The last the
woman saw was of Katie and Sonia turning round the
point there. They never came back.'

'Then the boy sounded the alarm?'

Derek nodded. 'Even if they were cut off by the tide it
would have been very shallow at first, almost a trickle,
but it fills rapidly without warning. In an hour Froggat's
Hole is just that, a hole in a cave cut off from the beach.'

Just then a police officer came over and explained that
a launch was going out to the entrance of the cave. Preston
asked if there were medical supplies aboard and was told
that there were, plus two divers and a member of the
rescue team who knew every inch of Froggat's Hole.

'I'll come with you,' he said at once, and Vanessa
gripped his arm.

'I'm coming too.' She glanced at the policeman. 'I'm
a nurse and I might be of help.'

The policeman glanced at Preston. 'Perhaps if you both
came. We can judge what's to be done when we're at sea.'

Vanessa gripped Preston's hand and he looked down at
her. 'All right,' he agreed reluctantly and, leaving the
Farnsworths, they went to the jetty.

The trip out took less than fifteen minutes. By the time
they arrived the long, flat stretch of sand, which was quite
accessible at low tide, was now covered by a swirling
greeny-blue water.

'That's Froggat's,' one of the team pointed out. A gap-
ing black hole in the cliffs looked out to the sea, washed
by white-tipped waves. 'The opening is large enough to
access by small boat but not by launch, of course. There
are three of the rescue team in there already with survival
gear and medical supplies. We're going to send the two
divers in now.'

'I'll go too,' Preston said at once.

'And if you've something I can change into. . .?' Vanessa insisted.

'We've wet suits below,' the man explained, 'but it's not going to be an easy ride into the mouth of the cave—'

'No,' interrupted Preston emphatically. 'Vanessa, I want you to stay here on the launch.'

'But what if I'm needed?' Vanessa shook her head. 'I'm trained medically for any situation that might arise, and I'm not afraid of the water.'

'I know,' he frowned, 'but that's not the point. I don't want you put at risk.'

She smiled. 'Thank you. But I shan't be. You'll be with me, won't you?'

To that there seemed no answer. He knew that she was a strong swimmer, should the need arise, and would not be discouraged easily. Eventually he ran a hand through his hair, shrugged and gave her a wry grin.

'I'm not going to stop you, am I?'

'No,' she whispered, 'I'm afraid you're stuck with me.'

Taking her hand, he tugged her behind him and they went below. They changed into wet suits and life-jackets while the small motor boat bobbed alongside and then they were helped into it once more. In the tiny craft Preston slid an arm around her shoulders. 'I've never met anyone so stubborn,' he complained, and hugged her tightly.

She huddled close to him as the wind blew in their faces. When they reached the shadow of the cliff the waters became choppy, and the boat ducked and dived with breathtaking precision as one of the divers piloted the way into the mouth of Froggat's Hole.

She was glad of Preston's strong body beside her, the power and strength of his limbs equal to those of the men in the boat who were trained for this kind of work. She felt a sudden surge of pride and leaned into him as the dark mouth of the cave loomed over them.

It was dim and echoing and the sea swelled up and

backward like a great sliding floor. Only a pinnacle of light in the distance reflected where the rescue team had made their camp.

The boat finally edged up to a ledge of rock, and the men threw ropes to the boat and tugged them in. Despite the precarious lifting and dropping of the boat, they were hauled to temporary safety.

Powerful battery arc lights lit up the greeny-black rock and the pile of equipment stacked there. The two divers went into consultation with the men who began strapping waterproof packages to their backs.

'Space blankets in sealed packs,' one of them explained. 'And medical supplies, food and drink.'

'How will you reach them?' Preston asked.

'The same way the youngster came out, with a bit of luck.' One of the divers called Ray pointed to a pool on the other side of the ledge. 'Down there, under the claw of rock and up into the cave on the other side.'

'You make it sound simple,' Preston observed wryly. 'Look, I can use an aqualung. I'll go with you.'

Ray frowned. 'Better find them first. If it's safe, you can go next journey.'

'I'll come too,' began Vanessa, only to be stopped by Preston's grim expression.

'Better not, miss,' warned the diver. 'However good a swimmer you are, there are treacherous currents under there. Let's wait and see what the divers find.'

A shiver went down her spine at the word, 'find'. She had to make herself not think about its meaning as she crouched beside Preston at the edge of the pool. The two divers in their black and orange suits disappeared into the water. A few bubbles surfaced and the lifeline bobbed underwater, indicating that the divers were progressing. Then came the wait when the line went still, and the eerie silence of the cave seemed to be almost as noisy as the ocean outside.

'We are at high tide, I assume?' Preston asked one of the team.

'Almost,' was the worrying reply, and Vanessa's heart sank.

'Don't worry, they'll be OK,' Preston murmured and slipped an arm around her shoulders.

Vanessa felt hypnotised by the dark water. What seemed an eternity later the shiny black head of a diver broke the surface again. Ray wrenched off his mask as they helped him onto the rock. When he managed a breath he explained that there were four stranded people, a couple in their fifties and a mother and daughter.

'Are they safe where they are for the moment?' Preston asked.

'As long as the water doesn't rise any higher. He glanced at his diver's watch. 'We've half an hour to go before the water stops rising.'

'There's no other way of getting them out?'

'Not unless we take them the way we went in and that's impossible. None of them swim, except the little girl who told us she has to swim for her physiotherapy.'

Preston smiled grimly. 'Katie has an autoimmune condition, a form of rheumatoid arthritis.'

The diver nodded. 'She's a plucky little thing. Telling Mum everything's going to be all right, but I don't like the look of her legs. They seem very swollen around the knees.'

Preston glanced at Vanessa. Then he drew a hand through his damp, dark hair. 'So, we've just got to hope the water doesn't rise in there?'

'That's about it. Oh, and one thing more, the chap's a diabetic. He needs his shot apparently.'

'Damn,' Preston groaned. 'Is there any insulin in the medical packs?'

'All here,' said one of the team and showed them a sealed medical back pack.

'Fine,' said Preston, and began to pull it on with the help of the diver.

'You're sure you're OK with this?' Ray asked. 'You don't suffer from claustrophobia or panic attacks?'

Preston shook his head and grinned. 'I'll make it, don't worry.'

Ray looked relieved. 'I'll give you one of the smaller air devices to use. Make sure you follow me and the line and be careful not to graze yourself or your pack on the rock.'

Preston nodded, adjusting his equipment. Catching Vanessa's horrified expression, he squeezed her hand. 'We'll need help when the water goes down so have everything to hand—and make sure you keep warm. Are you all right?'

She wanted to reach up and tell him that she was terrified for him. Instead, she nodded and managed a smile, and he bent briefly and brushed his lips against hers. 'Drink something warm, put a thermal around you and stop worrying,' he told her.

And soon he was gone, his tall, unfamiliar figure in the black suit disappearing like an eel below the surface of the pool.

'Soup?' someone offered, and she looked up to see one of the rescue team grinning at her. 'Go on, it'll do you good. And do as he says, don't worry. He'll be OK.'

She couldn't remember how long she sat there, warming her hands on the hot mug, nor how long afterwards it was that she and the other members of the team watched the water inch dangerously upward.

How was Sonia coping with the strain? she wondered. Only a few weeks ago she had been at her lowest. If Katie was in pain or had an attack which resulted in a fever, without warmth or air. . .

Much later, Vanessa realised she had almost drifted off to sleep as she huddled with her arms around her knees.

A fresh boat had pulled in and despatched new people and more supplies, including portable stretchers.

'Tide's ebbing,' someone shouted and Vanessa sat up and stared at the pool. It was going down. Little by little it was definitely receding from the rim, leaving a seaweedy frieze around the rocks' edges.

We can crawl down after it,' one of the divers told her. She saw that the rock splayed out like the inside of a shell, leaving slippery ridges all the way down the wall of the cave. 'The team can take the stretchers as soon as we begin to see the opening to the next cavern.'

'It's like an underwater maze!' Vanessa shuddered.

'Exactly what it is,' her companion agreed gloomily. 'Right, let's make a start, shall we?'

Eventually the level of the seawater dropped. It was astonishing to see the long slippery slope which began to reveal a path and then a dark entrance to yet another cave. Suddenly everyone was in motion, the team working to a practised routine as they followed in single file down the treacherous path and finally into the heart of the cave.

They squelched across sodden sand and shingle and Vanessa squinted. In suspense, she waited for the advance party to come back. Her heart leapt when she saw lights in the blackness.

If she could have run she would have, but her ankles were lost in the boggy quagmire of the cave floor. Preston came out of the gloom, his dark hair wet and his tall body unfamiliar in the diving suit.

'Hey, what's all this about?' he laughed softly as she hugged him.

'I thought. . .' she began, and shivered as he put an arm around her shoulders.

'Tell me later what you thought,' he whispered and kissed her with cold blue lips. 'Come on, we need to do a little tidying up.'

Which was, Vanessa decided, an understatement as she

discovered the scene on a small, precarious ledge. Katie and Sonia were wrapped in space blankets. Katie's little face was puffy and Vanessa opened a fresh sterile pack and began to bathe her eyes. Sonia was shaking and had a gash on her forehead.

Preston and the other men began to lift the diabetic man onto the stretcher. Though the swift injection of insulin he'd received had avoided a coma, he was looking sallow and his eyes were dull. His wife was in obvious agony with her ankle.

'How is she?' Vanessa asked Preston as they lifted her onto one of the stretchers.

'I gave her analgesics and strapped the ankle, but I think she has a nasty fracture there.'

'How long will it take to get to the beach?'

'About ten minutes, that's all. Through that tunnel of rock, which is the one they strayed through. It's no distance now the water's down. They've brought ambulances up to the end of the lane, and there's a police escort waiting to see them through to Fretmouth Cottage Hospital. Now, how are we doing here?'

Sonia's teeth were chattering. 'W-we're all right. But I'll n-never come to this place again,' she stammered.

The stretcher-bearers arrived and lifted Katie onto one and Sonia onto the second. As Vanessa followed alongside Katie the little girl held her hand and she squeezed it tightly. Katie looked pale and her eyes were swollen badly but, for all she'd been through, Vanessa thought what incredible spirit she had.

The rescue team and ambulance men ferried them into daylight. Derek and Gail Farnsworth ran across the sand to greet them, the relief obvious on their faces as Sonia tried to explain what had happened.

Vanessa rode in the ambulance with Katie and Sonia. 'Where's Dr Lynley?' Katie asked as the siren sounded above.

'He's gone with the man who is a diabetic,' Vanessa told her.

'He gave me something to stop my legs aching.' Katie blinked her puffy eyes. 'And he didn't let that man die either. I thought he was going to die when he went all funny on the rock.'

'Well, Dr Lynley's a pretty good doctor.' Vanessa tucked the blanket under the small chin.

'He's the best doctor in the world,' Katie giggled, and Vanessa nodded. He was, indeed. He hadn't cared about the risk to himself or what danger he was in. He hadn't hesitated when he'd known that he would have to swim into Froggat's Hole.

And after today, when she had waited for some news on that ledge—waited and prayed for him to come safely back to her—she must be mad to ever think that she could live without him, which, of course, was exactly what she was going to have to do in just over four short weeks' time.

CHAPTER ELEVEN

LUCKILY, Casualty was not busy in Fretmouth Cottage Hospital, though a few holiday-makers straggled along the corridors and made their way out into the car park. Once the ambulances had disgorged their patients Vanessa disappeared with an obliging student nurse to the staff cloakrooms and was lent a pair of jeans and a sweater from Lost Property, peeling off the wet suit she still hadn't had time to change.

She realised that Preston must have done the same thing because he appeared in the waiting-room in unfamiliar clothes—some baggy linen trousers and a crumpled mustard T-shirt.

'Ray lent them to me,' he grinned, and took her arm to sit her down in the waiting area. 'I'll get us a hot cup of coffee and then we'll go and see how they are.'

Vanessa sat still and watched him go, his broad shoulders swaying. Suddenly a dull weariness seemed to overtake her and she slumped back into the chair, barely conscious of other people coming and going.

'Here, drink this.' Preston pushed a warm polystyrene mug, full to the brim with coffee, into her hand.

She drank and was grateful for the warmth as the drink revived her. 'How was your diabetic man?' she asked.

'Not especially good. Leg cramps, blurred vision due to excess glucose in the eye and desperately thirsty—apart from feeling exhausted, which isn't surprising after his ordeal.'

'What was he doing in the cave?'

'He's a retired geologist. He and his wife are here on a week's holiday after a summer cold he's had. They didn't realise how far they'd walked; didn't have any insulin with them, and seemed to be unaware that after a cold he's more vulnerable than ever.'

Vanessa sighed as she thought of just how close the man had come to lapsing into a coma, had not Preston reached him. 'Rummaging around in caves for rock pieces was about the last thing he needed to be doing this week in his condition.'

'Still, now we've got him here I don't think there's any doubt he'll make a recovery.'

'And his wife?'

'Nasty ankle fracture, I'm afraid. She's across the hall from A and E in X-Ray. They'll take her over to the plaster-room afterwards, I expect. She's still in shock; can't remember how she fell, but otherwise she's OK.'

Vanessa sipped her coffee and leant back. 'So it's just Sonia's head to be stitched and Katie to be checked?'

He nodded. 'I wouldn't be surprised if they keep Sonia in overnight because of the head wound and the possibility of concussion. Katie will probably stay too. Let's go and have a look, shall we?'

Wearily she got to her feet and followed Preston past Orthopaedics to the treatment room, where Sonia lay on one of the couches. The registrar on duty had just finished examining her.

'Well, nothing we can't patch up, Mrs Searle,' he was saying, 'but I'd like to keep you in for observation overnight, and Katie too.' He turned to introduce himself to Preston, and Vanessa talked to Sonia for a while—promising that she would ring Derek and Gail, who were waiting at home for news.

Having allayed Sonia's worries, they said a brief hello to Katie who was in the next cubicle playing with a doll one of the nurses had found for her.

'I'm staying in hospital with Mummy,' she told them proudly. 'And my eyes feel much better now, and my legs.'

Vanessa perched on the bed. 'You were a very brave girl today, Katie.'

Katie giggled up at Preston. 'Dr Lynley told me all about mermaids and the king who lives under the sea. But he didn't come up while I was there.'

Everyone laughed, but when Katie gave a massive yawn they slipped away whilst she snuggled down on the pillow with her doll.

Outside, in the waiting area, Vanessa rang Gail and Derek who assured her that they would be there tomorrow to collect Sonia and Katie and take them back for the rest of their holiday.

Which suddenly made Vanessa think of her own holiday as she replaced the receiver and walked back to Preston. He rubbed a large hand over his face and blinked.

'I was just thinking. . .' Vanessa began, and then glanced at her watch. 'Do you know it's a quarter past nine?'

'I've stopped counting,' he groaned wearily, drawing her into his arms. It was so good just to be close to him once more; to feel his solid heartbeat against her breast. 'And we've yet to find a hotel somewhere along the banks of the river Dart.'

She looked up into his tired face. 'I'd rather we drove home.'

He gave her a frown. 'You're serious?'

She realised that she could not say there would always be another day. No, she was fully aware that their holiday would never take place. 'I want to go home,' she whispered, looking up at him.

'If it's the driving, we could stay here. . .go on in the morning,' he suggested considerately. 'Drive back early Monday morning. . .'

She shook her head and made a brave effort to smile.

'No,' she whispered and felt his lips softly brush her forehead in silent agreement.

Vanessa gloried in the wonderful sensation of hot water trickling down her back and over her bottom to cascade in rivulets over her thighs, sending all the little particles of residual sand down into the base of the shower and into the waste. Her long, wet hair clung to her skin as she lifted her face in the warm water, only just beginning to feel the warmth penetrate her cold limbs.

At least she had stopped shaking. Though, as she let the water rush over her face, she wasn't sure if the shaking was due to extreme tiredness or perhaps the disappointment of her doomed weekend.

She reached out to turn off the water and a hand went over her fingers. A hard wall of muscle attached itself to her naked body.

'Is there room for two?'

She flicked open her eyes. Wet male skin dazzled her. A glistening head of black hair scraped back from a newly shaved face came down and lips began to nibble her neck.

'Did you phone the hotel?' she managed shakily.

'I think they had some doubt as to whether I was telling the truth. As a matter of fact, the truth sounded pretty hopeless—even to me.'

'Saving people trapped on a ledge in a particularly gloomy cave isn't the usual run-of-the-mill excuse,' she murmured softly, trying to ignore the rioting sensations within her body. 'Are you terribly shattered?'

'No.' He dragged his fingers through her wet hair. 'Not too shattered. . .not for you.' She gave a little gasp as he pulled her to him. 'Do you see what you're doing to me, woman?'

She hauled in a gasp of air as he kissed her throat. 'Turn around. Let me rub your shoulders.' He did as she suggested and she slid the pads of her thumbs over the tense muscle which was knotted with tension after the swim into the pool of the cave. As he sighed with pleasure she smoothed her fingers along the tanned valley of skin between his shoulder-blades.

'What's next?' he murmured as she moved behind him to ladle shower gel over the broad shoulders and strong hips which had accomplished so much today. Not a great many men would have done what he had done. The prospect of an underwater dive in those conditions would have seemed terrifying to most people. She had listened to the rescue team while they waited on that rocky platform. They had been full of admiration for a man who was untrained in their acquired skills.

He turned under the soapy water and wrapped his arms around her. 'You were wonderful.' he said, echoing her thoughts about him. 'A stubborn little witch, but wonderful all the same.'

'I didn't do anything, except wait. You wouldn't let me swim into the Hole with you.'

'Only because. . .' He stopped, letting the water fountain over them. 'I know you would have managed it,' he said, seeming to change his mind. 'Now turn around and let me smother you in this stuff.'

She did as she was told. What had he been going to say? she wondered. Not that she wondered for long, as his touch over her body was too erotic to concentrate on anything but the breathtaking thud he was provoking in her heart. She swallowed, closing her eyes and leaning against him, and allowed herself full measure of the attention he was lavishing on her.

Two large hands slid from the smooth surface of her waist, melted across her breasts and brought their little pink buds erect. He smoothed away the lather and fluttered slow fingers over her hips and downward. When he reached her thighs he was driving her wild and she spun wetly in his arms, unable to stifle her groan of need.

Whether they had made love with the water on or off, she was never certain afterwards. All she could remember was the urgency with which he'd taken her and her equal intensity as she'd eventually collapsed against him, their bodies wet, arms and legs trembling as the sound of the water receded and left them panting in one another's arms.

He carried her from the shower and wrapped her in a warm towel. Then he draped one around himself and they lay in quiet harmony on the bed, her body consumed with a wonderful peace. She only knew that she wanted this feeling to go on for ever.

She also knew that it could not.

But she closed her eyes and refused to think of the morning, falling into a deep, deep sleep in the warm, strong circle of his arms.

Charlie sat down in the lounge and twinkled a hand on her knees.

Literally twinkled.

Vanessa—who was sitting opposite trying to read a book—felt rather than saw Charlie's grin spread all over her face, then her eyes fell to the two sparkling diamonds set in a silver clasp on Charlie's finger which she wiggled conspicuously.

'Charlie!' Vanessa sat bolt upright, dropping her book. 'What's that on your finger?'

'Do you like it?'

Vanessa stared at the beautiful engagement ring. 'Like it?' She looked up in amazement. 'Why, it's wonderful! But when? How?'

Charlie burst into laughter. 'You idiot. It's been sitting on my finger for weeks ever since you and Preston—' She giggled and blushed. 'Do you remember I told you I had some news to tell you when we next met?'

Vanessa rolled her eyes heavenward. 'But we never did, did we?'

'Not until you were going away, and you were too excited to notice.'

'Oh, I'm sorry, Charlie! I must have been blind. I'm so happy for you and Ken.'

'But you didn't expect it?' Charlie asked with an amused glint in her blue eyes. 'Obviously not enough to notice a ring on my finger?'

Vanessa hesitated. 'Well, I know what your career means to you and you must love Ken very much. . .'

Charlie lifted wry brows. 'I suppose I must. I just know that when he proposed I said yes. He didn't have to ask me twice.'

'I'm so happy for you, Charlie.'

Her friend stared at her under her lashes. 'You've only a couple of weeks left to go at the practice, haven't you?'

Vanessa sighed, wondering where the time had gone. August had passed brutally quickly after the Fretmouth episode. Now they were well into September. She stared wistfully at Charlie's amazing engagement ring. 'I'm leaving the surgery on the last Friday of September, and I'll spend the next week just getting my stuff ready to take up to London.'

'What about Preston?' Charlie asked. 'Couldn't you still come back at weekends?'

'With his schedule and mine?' Vanessa cupped her chin in her hands. 'It just wouldn't work, Charlie. You just can't hold onto people at a distance. It would be unfair on both of us if we tried.'

'But do you love him?'

Vanessa's mouth quirked slightly. 'It's not as simple as that.'

'Van, why won't you admit you love him? If you do, then you're making the biggest mistake of your life in leaving him.'

'And if it's no?'

'If it's no, then you're probably doing the best thing in going to London.'

'But for all I know he's pleased our affair is over.'

'Do you really think that?'

Vanessa looked miserably down into her lap and thought of Caroline Grey. She'd heard that the affair with Mike was over. And it had not escaped her notice that Preston had spent a great deal of time with Caroline lately.

'You've two weeks left,' Charlie reminded her unnecessarily. 'For heaven's sake, don't let your pride get in the way. Go to him. Tell him you love him. Tell him you've changed your mind.'

'I wish I could,' Vanessa said, realising how much she meant it. Had it been wishful thinking when he'd stopped short in his sentence that day? When she had wondered if he was going to say that he really cared? But, then, if he thought anything of her he wouldn't let her go.

Charlie got up, went to the bedroom and came back with Vanessa's sweater and shoulder-bag. She pushed them into her hands, pulled her up off the sofa and marched her to the door. 'Preston!' she ordered. 'And spill the beans!'

Vanessa found herself starting the car and then switching off the engine. She looked awful. Her hair was a mess. She should really have it trimmed, it was so wild and untamed. She could do nothing about it spilling over her face.

She wore no make-up and yet her grey eyes seemed huge and moist with apprehension as she stared into the driving mirror. There were smudges of black beneath them from the nights she had been unable to sleep—as she'd lain awake, convincing herself that she couldn't wait to start her new job.

How could she possibly walk up to his front door and tell him how she felt?

Could she stand the silent, pregnant pause as he digested the implications of such a statement and offered in return an ambiguous answer? She could not imagine that he would simply sweep her into his arms and say that he would now rearrange his life to suit her—a life that might well include Caroline Grey!

Besides, it was Saturday afternoon, he was on call and he was probably out on a visit. In which case, why was she worrying? If the Porsche wasn't parked at the front of the house then the problem was solved. She wouldn't have enough courage to call again and by Monday, when she saw him in surgery, sanity would have returned.

Vanessa drove slowly, her heart racing. When she turned into Preston's road and cast an eye along it she saw the Porsche, sitting sleekly by the kerb. She didn't know whether to be relieved or disappointed or, quite simply, terrified.

She pulled up behind it and sat in silence. If she went home she would have to face Charlie. If she rang the bell. . .?

Now that she had come this far, she must! The thought of wrapping her arms around him and melting into his strong body made her tremble with anticipatory greed. If she kissed him, felt his mouth cover hers, looked into those green eyes—everything else would come naturally. . .

Her feet flew over the pavement and up the four neat white steps to the Georgian front door. She barely hesitated as she pressed the bell. She did not have to wait long. The door slowly opened and she took a step forward, eager to throw herself into his arms and tell him she loved him.

'Vanessa!' gasped a soft, constrained voice.

And Vanessa stood in numbed silence as Caroline Grey, dressed in Preston's towelling robe and very little else, opened the door cautiously.

CHAPTER TWELVE

CAROLINE GREY drew the collar of the towelling robe around her neck, inching back on the polished floor with bare feet. 'Come in, won't you?' she murmured, her voice husky, but Vanessa stayed where she was—somehow dredging up a smile.

'No, it's not important,' she refused politely, aware that her voice seemed to be incredibly unchanged and not distorted by the rapid pounding of blood in her ears. 'I've come at an inconvenient time.'

Caroline Grey brushed back her dark hair, revealing flushed cheeks. Her eyes still looked sleepy, as if she had stumbled from bed to the door in a state of confusion.

'It's not important,' Vanessa said again. 'I'll see Pres. . . Dr Lynley some other time.' She managed to stumble her way back down the white steps, offering a shaky but fairly audible goodbye as she hurried back to her car.

Tears filled her eyes as she slammed the door. Fumbling her way out of the space behind the Porsche, she squealed her way onto the road. By the time she allowed herself to think about what had happened her nose was red and her box of tissues on the seat beside her empty. She took long, painful breaths of air from the open window.

It hurt so much. The pain was overwhelming.

Of course, she had suspected all along but she had chosen to ignore the signs. No wonder he hadn't tried to persuade her to stay in Brideport! What other reason could there be but Caroline?

The tears smarted on her cheeks and she swept them away angrily. She had been a fool in more ways than one.

Again the sickening feeling of being deceived came back
to haunt her.

Slowly she dredged up the courage to ask herself why.
She was sensible enough to know that there were two
sides to every story, even this. In all fairness, she had told
him that her career meant everything. She had given him
no reason to think that she would change her mind about
her future so she had no claim on him emotionally.

Even so. . .the sight of Caroline in his robe begged an
obvious question. How long had Caroline and Preston
been lovers?

A question to which Charlie rapidly supplied the answer
when she returned home. 'It's just not like Preston to do
something so mean,' Charlie sighed, sinking beside her
on the sofa. 'Anyway, I thought Caroline and Mike Shelley
were the two involved.'

Vanessa closed her eyes as she rested her head back on
the cushions. 'They were. But I can't deny what I saw
with my own eyes.'

Charlie shrugged. 'There could be some other explanation.'

'Like what?' Vanessa waited but Charlie could provide
no reasonable explanation.

'You're just guessing,' Charlie settled for, uncon-
vincingly.

'Charlie, she was standing there in his robe. She had
bare feet and she looked—well, she didn't look as if she
was just visiting. What was I supposed to think?'

Charlie sighed. 'I don't know, Van. But I think you
should see Preston before you jump to conclusions.'

Vanessa shook her head. 'I don't want to see him. I
don't want to go back to the surgery. . .not now.'

'But you've two weeks left!'

'They can find someone easily enough—from the same
agency that they used to find me. Or perhaps Caroline's

sister is ready to fill the post. I'm going to phone Beth now and let her know.'

'But what will you say?'

Vanessa shrugged miserably. 'I'll think of something.'

'Isn't that a coward's way out?'

Vanessa looked down at her hands clenched together in her lap and nodded. 'Maybe. But what purpose will it serve if I walk into the surgery on Monday? Apart from my patients, who are booked in and who can very well be seen by an agency nurse for two weeks, all it would do is cause embarrassment. I don't think I could stand it.' She looked up at Charlie with glistening grey eyes. 'Think about it, Charlie. I spoke to Caroline early this morning. It's now past teatime. If Preston had wanted to talk to me he wouldn't have let a day slip by, would he? As far as I'm concerned, it's better like this.'

Charlie frowned. 'Well, you're being very philosophical about it, I must say. If it were me I'd demand an explanation.'

And what good would that do? Vanessa asked herself miserably. She had seen enough this morning to know that Caroline Grey meant more to Preston than he had ever truthfully revealed. Not that she had any right to judge him—he had taken her, Vanessa, at face value. She had told him that she was moving on to a new life and he had accepted her at her word.

Perhaps that was what hurt so much.

The phone rang several times that evening, and it was Preston. Charlie answered it and made an excuse that Vanessa was out. The next morning, Sunday, Vanessa phoned Beth at home and apologised for the inconvenience, explaining that she wouldn't be in on Monday and that they would have to find someone to take her place. Beth assumed that she was not well and Vanessa didn't bother to dispel the impression. It would be simpler all round if she was off sick. Simpler for everyone.

The phone rang on Monday evening, and it was Preston. Vanessa picked it up, thinking that it was Charlie from the hospital. Her heart pounded as she heard his voice.

'Are you really sick?' he demanded.

'I'm not coming back to work,' she told him.

'But you've two weeks left—'

'You know why,' she told him shortly.

'The hell I do!' His voice was furious. 'What's all this about, Vanessa? Charlie's been fobbing me off with pathetic excuses, and now you tell me you're not coming back to work!'

'Do you really expect me to?' she blurted out, her cheeks blazing.

'Of course I do. What the—' The line went dead. She listened to the dialling tone, her heart racing. What excuse was he about to give her, she wondered as tears of unbearable hurt brimmed in her eyes. She sank down and tried to think. She seemed to be shaking inside and out. She felt sick and light-headed, as though delayed shock was coming out.

Five minutes later the intercom demanded to be answered. 'Let me up,' he told her through the microphone.

'I don't want to see you.' Her voice was shaky with emotion. 'Please go away.'

'Let me up, or I shall start shouting on the front lawn.'

'Preston. . .go away. Please.'

'Not until you tell me what's wrong.'

She finally gave in and allowed him entrance to the flats. In seconds he had leapt the stairs and was at the door. When she opened it he stared at her, his mouth clamped into a straight line.

'There's no point in this,' she told him, her voice cracking. 'We've nothing left to say to each other.'

'Oh, haven't we?' He pushed past her. He looked so

good in a chocolate linen shirt and dark trousers. His green eyes glittered angrily.

When she'd closed the door she lifted her chin and stared at him. 'If it's about finding a replacement—'

'No, it's not about another bloody replacement,' he growled at her, 'and you know damn well it isn't. It's about us. Why have you avoided me since Saturday?'

'You know why.'

'Suppose you tell me, even so?'

She felt her eyes smarting and she dropped her gaze, pushing back her hair with trembling hands. 'You owe me nothing, Preston. We didn't make each other any promises.'

'Which was your idea, not mine,' he reminded her brusquely. 'You wanted a cut and dried finish to our relationship but, my God, I didn't think you'd do it like this!'

'Me!' she exclaimed, two stripes of crimson running down her cheeks.

'Do you realise how many times I've had to stop myself from begging you not to go? How many times I told myself that I would be trapping you into a life you didn't want— even if I managed to persuade you into staying in Brideport? Have you given it any thought at all that it might not have been so easy for me as it was for you to meet your wretched deadline and just turn off my emotions?'

Vanessa stared at him in amazement. 'How can you say that?' Her breath caught in her throat.

'Easily, since I have a heart and it's capable of being wounded—even though you don't appear to think so!'

She could not believe this. He was telling her that he was wounded—after what she had seen? 'How do you think I felt,' she hurled at him fiercely, 'when I arrived on your doorstep on Saturday morning and found Caroline Grey standing there? Preston, she was dressed in your robe! What was I supposed to do then? Make an appointment to see you when you were not—' she searched for the right word, a word which would hurt him as much as she was hurting right now, but all she could find to come up with was a pathetic '—occupied?'

He stared at her for a long, penetrating moment. She met his gaze unwaveringly until finally his brow creased and he took a breath. 'You came to my house on Saturday morning?'

She almost laughed. But she nearly. . .very nearly. . . cried instead as a mistiness began to creep over her eyes. 'I think you had better go,' she mumbled, afraid that she was about to collapse into tears.

'I didn't know,' he began, reaching out to take hold of her. 'Vanessa. . .I didn't know.' His expression darkened. 'Damn it, you think Caroline and I—?'

She wriggled out of his grasp. 'Please go,' she managed, holding on to her last vestiges of pride.

Green eyes chilled to ice. He straightened his body, pulling back the broad shoulders. 'No, you don't, do you? Because, if you did, you might hear something that might make you realise just what you're throwing away. And who am I to interfere with your career strategy—your perfect plan for the future—which excludes all forms of close human relationships?' He turned and walked to the door, pulling it open with an angry jerk.

'Well, as far as I'm concerned, if you were prepared to think so badly of me without giving me the opportunity to explain then I think you've probably done the wisest thing. Hospital management certainly knew what they were doing when they hired you!'

If she had thought that she was hurting before, she had not really known what it felt like until now. Alone in the flat, with the faint scent of his aftershave hanging in the air, she sank to the sofa and buried her head in her hands.

*   *   *

It was a glorious Sunday in October when Charlie helped Vanessa cram her luggage into the Citroën. Charlie was off in a week's time to her Spanish holiday with Ken. She wrapped her arms around Vanessa and hugged her. 'I'll send you a postcard from Palma,' she said, and Vanessa hugged her back.

'Send it to the hospital. I'll be staying temporarily in the nurses' accommodation.'

'You must be mad! London in the rain and the nurses' hostel! Lord, I don't envy you, Vanessa. Come with Ken and me to Spain.'

They giggled. 'Don't tempt me,' laughed Vanessa softly, and climbed into the car. 'Take care,' she murmured, and felt a dangerous prickle of wetness behind her eyes as she stuck her hand out of the window. 'I'll write.'

She swallowed deeply as she drove away, watching Charlie's figure in the driving mirror for the last time as she drove out of Chandler's Row. There were still two calls she had to make on her way out of Brideport. Howarth Rd and the General. She stopped first at Sonia's, knocked on the door and was greeted with open arms by Katie.

'I don't want you to go,' Katie cried as she sat on her lap in the kitchen.

'Come to see me when you visit London,' Vanessa cajoled, trying to sound breezy, but her heart was aching. She'd made true friends with Katie and Sonia and she would miss them.

They all hugged at the door when she left. Sonia was looking fitter and was coping with Katie's flare-ups, which made Vanessa feel better, but as she drove off her heart grew heavier. Now that she was leaving Brideport for ever she knew what she was going to lose. The sea, the town, its people, her friends, her roots. How right Charlie's grandmother had been when she'd warned, 'Be careful what you wish for. . .'

And—there was Preston. Not a word in two weeks. Oh,

she had missed him so bitterly. There was a deep, empty chasm inside her which ate up any enthusiasm she had for life. How she missed his strong body and presence in her life, his humour and his kindness, and how it was even harder to believe now that he had deceived her.

Vanessa brought the car to a halt in the hospital car park, and walked to the lake. Francesca and Gary were sitting on their usual bench, waiting for her. When Sister Miles had phoned her to say that Francesca had changed her mind and was staying Vanessa had suspected that it might have something do with a promising new relationship.

She gazed into Francesca's happy face and knew that real love had come into her life. 'I'm staying until I reach eight stones—that's my target weight,' Francesca told her. She glanced at Gary, who nodded.

'Me too. We've decided to crack this thing together, reach our target weights and then. . .' he took hold of Francesca's hand '. . .we're going to start afresh.'

It was the best going-away news Vanessa could have received. She was so happy for Francesca. Eventually she left them, promising to keep in touch. She made her way, for the last time also, from Duncrey Ward to the car park.

Just as she arrived at the Citroën a slight figure emerged from the car parked next to hers.

'Vanessa?' Caroline Grey walked towards her.

Vanessa's heart quickened. She wished that she still felt angry, but all she felt was a great emptiness and an almost unbearable sadness.

'Have you a minute to spare?' she asked.

Vanessa shook her head. 'I'm just leaving for London.'

Caroline Grey sighed. 'Look, I must explain something. The day you came to Preston's house I'd slept there over-night, but it was only the once—'

'Please. . .' Vanessa fumbled for her keys '. . .I'd rather not—'

Caroline put a restraining hand on her arm. 'I slept—in his guest room—because I was in such a terrible state the night before. I'd gone to Preston to explain that I'd decided to end the practice partnership. Mike is going back to his wife and boys. I'm the one who's going, Vanessa, not Mike.' Her eyes were full of pain as she talked.

'I was close to breaking point and Preston couldn't get much sense out of me. He gave me a sedative and I just flaked out. The next morning, when you called, Preston was working in the garden and I answered the door. I know what it must have looked like. . .but I still felt drugged. I dropped back into bed after you went, forgetting to tell Preston that you'd called.'

Vanessa shook her head slowly, trying to understand. 'But I thought—'

'That Preston and I were lovers?' Caroline gave a deep sigh. 'I wish I could have fallen in love with someone like Preston, but the only man for me is Mike. That's why I'm going away. I'd destroy his marriage if I stayed. I've decided to go abroad—it's the only solution for me.'

Vanessa put her hand to her head. 'Then you and Preston—'

'We're just good friends, to use that dreadful cliché. But it's true. We've never regarded each other as anything but friends.'

What kind of terrible mistake had she made? Vanessa asked herself as she reached out to steady herself.

'Go to him, Vanessa,' Caroline said softly. 'Swallow your pride. It's still not too late.'

Her thoughts were in a whirl as she drove. She'd been so determined not to let his love enter her heart. And why? Because she was scared of love. Of its responsibilities and its burdens. Of its pain.

She'd replaced Tara and Dad with a career in hospital management, knowing that if she opened herself fully to loving again she might be hurt. She had tried to separate herself from the emotions which she had refused to contemplate since her mother's death. But living a life without any of them, including pain and heartache, meant that you were not really living at all.

Was it too late? Had she thrown away her chance of happiness with the only man she had ever loved?

Her body shook as she drew up at the house. The Porsche was parked at the kerb.

Did she have the courage? Then suddenly she thought of Caroline and her poor, pain-racked face and of the doomed affair with Mike and the courage it must have taken to end both the practice partnership and her relationship.

She managed to climb out of the car and walk to the pavement. She climbed the steps hesitantly, put out her hand and stopped—he had every right to tell her to go away, just as she had told him.

Could she face such tortuous rejection, knowing that she had been the one to blame all along? She pressed the bell, as she had done two weeks ago—and waited.

After a while the door opened. He wore old garden shorts and thongs and very little else. She felt heady with need and love and she stared into the green eyes which, for a moment, regarded her with painful, detached scrutiny.

She wanted to say so much. Yet she didn't know where to begin. Why should he bother listening? She had hurt him; she knew that now. She had wounded him deeply on that terrible Monday.

'Preston. . .I was wrong,' she heard herself trying to apologise. 'Wrong from the beginning. I'm so sorry. I'm so dreadfully sorry. And I wouldn't blame you if you shut the door in my face—'

'Wouldn't you?' he said in a gravel voice which made her feel that all her fears were about to come true.

'I've just spoken to Caroline,' she faltered, her heart pounding. 'She told me what happened.'

'As I could have told you—and wanted to tell you.'

She gave a choked little sob and nodded. Then, as she closed her eyes and pictured herself walking away down the steps, the breath almost went out of her body as he took her wrist and pulled her into the house.

'You look terrible,' he told her bluntly as he took her in his arms. 'I hope you've suffered as much as I have.'

He kissed her startled mouth and she felt her strength ebb away and melt into him as she wrapped her arms around his neck and heard, vaguely, the door slam behind them.

She heard or saw very little else after that. Her vision was full of the man she loved as they somehow clambered up to the bedroom. All she knew was that, after dispensing with her jeans and blouse and his own singular piece of clothing, he tugged her towards him and began to demolish her as if he had been starved for weeks. Which, she thought later, in a sense they had been.

His love-making was intense, yet forgiving. She felt tears of happiness run down her cheeks as she lay in his arms. Did anyone have a right to feel like this? she wondered as her body throbbed from the pleasure he gave her.

'Now tell me,' he whispered as he stroked her tangle of coppery hair from her face and kissed the soft skin behind her ear. 'Have you missed me?'

She swallowed, nodding, sliding her fingers over the tanned brown muscle and trembling at the magic beneath her touch. 'Missed you; ached for you; wanted you.'

'So will you tell me why you wouldn't believe me about Caroline?'

She bit down on her lip, pressing her face into his chest until he brought up her chin to meet his gaze. 'I was upset. . .' she offered tamely.

He crooked an eyebrow. 'Because you were jealous.'

'No. . .' She blushed. 'Yes, yes. If you must know, I
was consumed with jealousy.'

He smiled at her tenderly. 'A perfectly understandable
reaction for someone who is in love. But, then, I don't
know if—'

She leaned forward to kiss the words from his lips. 'You
know,' she whispered, 'you know I love you.'

He was silent for a moment and she felt him shudder.
Then he hugged her until she could hardly breathe. 'Oh,
darling, I thought I'd never hear you say it. I wanted to
say I loved you so often. I nearly choked in stopping
myself. I was terrified I would scare you away, or I would
hear myself grovelling; hear myself trying to change
you and knowing it wouldn't work. Not if you didn't
really want me to love you.' He leaned on one elbow and
looked down at her. 'I love you, Vanessa. I've loved you
always.'

She stroked back his dark, thick hair and wondered just
how crazy she had been over the last six months to imagine
life without him. 'I don't want to go away, Preston. I want
to stay, if you'll have me.'

He looked deeply into her grey, love-filled eyes. 'I've
no intention of allowing you to escape me this time.'

'Promise?'

'My first promise. . .in this bed. The other promises. . .
come later. When I see you standing beside me in a church.
When I can lift the veil and look down at your lovely face
and slip a ring on your finger and call you my wife. When
you'll be fully mine. That's what I want, Vanessa.'

'Oh, sweetheart, that's what I want too.'

He cupped her face in his hands. 'You're sure?'

'Oh, yes, I'm sure.' She pulled him down beside her as
the Sunday bells pealed out over Brideport. 'First thing
tomorrow I'm going to ask for my old job back,' she
teased softly, 'if my employers haven't found someone
else to take my place.'

'No one ever could,' he told her, bringing his mouth down over her waiting lips. 'The practice has missed you,' he whispered, 'especially one partner in particular. . .'

And he began to show her exactly what he meant.

MILLS & BOON®

Medical Romance™

COMING NEXT MONTH

THE PERFECT WIFE AND MOTHER?
by Caroline Anderson
Audley Memorial Hospital

Ryan O'Connor wanted a lover. No commitment, no ties. And Ginny Jeffries agreed, against her better judgement, to accept Ryan O'Connor's terms. But being his lover meant deepening ties with Ryan and his two small children, and all she could see ahead was heartbreak...

INTIMATE PRESCRIPTION by Margaret Barker

Adam Lennox was surprised to see that Trisha Redman was a mother. Eight years previously she had refused to marry him because she was fearful of a physical relationship. So how could she enjoy a physical relationship with another man? Would Trisha tell Adam the truth?

PROMISE OF A MIRACLE by Marion Lennox
Gundowring Hospital

Meg Preston's quiet visit to Gundowring took an unexpected turn when she fell into the path—and home—of Rob Daniels. Before she knew it she was bound up in the Gundowring way of life and was falling in love with Rob! But Meg had a fiancé waiting in England...

WINNING THROUGH by Laura MacDonald

Dr Harry Brolin forecast that Kirstin Patterson would only survive one month as a GP in his tough inner city practice. She soon proved that she could handle even the most perilous of situations. But could she handle her dangerous feelings for Harry?

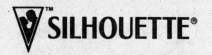

▼ SILHOUETTE®

Tempting...Tantalising...Terrifying!

Strangers in the night

Three spooky love stories in one compelling volume by three masters of the genre:

Dark Journey by Anne Stuart
Catching Dreams by Chelsea Quinn Yarbro
Beyond Twilight by Maggie Shayne

Available: July 1997   Price: £4.99

SUMMER SEARCH

How would you like to win a year's supply of Mills & Boon® books? Well you can and they're FREE! Simply complete the competition below and send it to us by 31st December 1997. The first five correct entries picked after the closing date will each win a year's subscription to the Mills & Boon series of their choice. What could be easier?

SPADE

SUNSHINE

PICNIC

BEACHBALL

SWIMMING

SUNBATHING

CLOUDLESS

FUN

TOWEL

SAND

HOLIDAY

W	Q	T	U	H	S	P	A	D	E	M	B
E	Q	R	U	O	T	T	K	I	U	I	E
N	B	G	H	L	H	G	O	D	W	K	A
I	I	O	A	I	N	E	S	W	Q	L	C
H	N	U	N	D	D	F	W	P	E	O	H
S	U	N	B	A	T	H	I	N	G	L	B
N	S	E	A	Y	F	C	M	D	A	R	A
U	B	P	K	A	N	D	M	N	U	T	L
S	E	N	L	I	Y	B	I	A	N	U	L
H	B	U	C	K	E	T	N	S	N	U	E
T	A	E	W	T	O	H	G	H	O	T	F
C	L	O	U	D	L	E	S	S	P	W	N

C7F

Please turn over for details of how to enter ☞

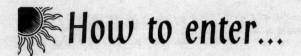# How to enter...

Hidden in the grid are eleven different summer related words. You'll find the list beside the word puzzle overleaf and they can be read backwards, forwards, up, down and diagonally. As you find each word, circle it or put a line through it. When you have found all eleven, don't forget to fill in your name and address in the space provided below and pop this page in an envelope (you don't even need a stamp) and post it today. Hurry competition ends 31st December 1997.

Mills & Boon Summer Search Competition
FREEPOST, Croydon, Surrey, CR9 3WZ
EIRE readers send competition to PO Box 4546, Dublin 24.

Please tick the series you would like to receive if you are a winner
Presents™ ❏   Enchanted™ ❏   Temptation® ❏
Medical Romance™ ❏   Historical Romance™ ❏

Are you a Reader Service™ Subscriber?   Yes ❏   No ❏

Ms/Mrs/Miss/Mr _____

(BLOCK CAPS PLEASE)

Address _____

_____

_____ Postcode _____

(I am over 18 years of age)